A Man Lay Dead

Dame Ngaio Marsh was born in New Zealand in 1895 and died in February 1982. She wrote over 30 detective novels and many of her stories have theatrical settings, for Ngaio Marsh's real passion was the theatre. She was both actress and producer and almost single-handedly revived the New Zealand public's interest in the theatre. It was for this work that she received what she called her 'damery' in 1966.

NGAIO MARSH

A MAN LAY DEAD

HarperCollins*Publishers*

For
My Father
and in memory of
My Mother

HarperCollins*Publishers*
77-85 Fulham Palace Road
Hammersmith, London W6 8JB
www.**harpercollins**.co.uk

This paperback edition published 2000

First published in Great Britain by
Geoffrey Bles 1934

Copyright Ngaio Marsh 1934

ISBN 9780007944682

Set in Baskerville

CONTENTS

CHAPTER 1

'And there were Present . . .'

Nigel Bathgate, in the language of his own gossip column, was 'definitely intrigued' about his weekend at Frantock. At twenty-five he had outgrown that horror of enthusiasm which is so characteristic of youth-grown-up. He was actually on his way to Frantock, and in 'colossal form' at the very thought of it. They were doing it in such grandeur, too! He leant back in his first-class corner seat and grinned at his cousin opposite. Odd sort of fellow, old Charles. One never knew much of what went on behind that long dark mask of his. Good-looking bloke, too; women adored him, reflected Nigel, mentally wagging his head — still flattered and made up to him although he was getting on in years . . . forty-six or -seven.

Charles Rankin returned his young cousin's ruminative stare with one of those twisted smiles that always reminded Nigel of a faun.

'Shan't be long now,' said Rankin. 'The next station is ours. You can see the beginnings of Frantock over there to the left.'

Nigel stared across the patchwork landscape of little fields and hillocks to where a naked wood, fast, fast asleep in its wintry solitude, half hid the warmth of old brick.

'That's the house,' said Rankin.

'Who will be there?' asked Nigel, not for the first time. He had heard much of Sir Hubert Handesley's 'unique and delightfully original house-parties', from a brother journalist who had returned from one of them, if the truth be told, somewhat persistently enthusiastic. Charles Rankin, himself a connoisseur of house-parties, had refused many extremely enviable invitations in favour of these unpretentious weekends. And now, as the result of a dinner-party at old Charles's flat, here was Nigel himself about to be initiated. So: 'Who will be there?' asked Nigel again.

'The usual crowd, I suppose,' answered Rankin patiently, 'with the addition of one Doctor Foma Toka-reff, who dates, I imagine, from Handesley's Embassy days in Petrograd. There will be the Wildes, of course—they must be somewhere on the train. He's Arthur Wilde, the archaeologist. Marjorie Wilde is . . . rather attractive, I think. And I suppose Angela North. You've met her?'

'She's Sir Hubert's niece, isn't she? Yes, she dined that night at your flat with him.'

'So she did. If I remember, you seemed to get on rather pleasantly.'

'Will Miss Grant be there?' asked Nigel.

Charles Rankin stood up and struggled into his over-coat.

'Rosamund?' he said 'Yes, she'll be there.'

'What an extraordinarily expressionless voice old Charles has got,' reflected Nigel, as the train clanked into the little station and drew up with a long, steamy sigh.

The upland air struck chill after the stale stuffiness of the train. Rankin led the way out into a sunken country lane, where they found a group of three muffled passengers talking noisily while a chauffeur stowed luggage away into a six-seater Bentley.

'Hullo, Rankin,' said a thin, bespectacled man; 'thought you must be on the train.'

'I looked out for you at Paddington, Arthur,' rejoined Rankin. 'Have you met my cousin, all of you? Nigel Bathgate . . . Mrs Wilde . . . Mr Wilde. Rosamund, you have met, haven't you?'

Nigel had made his bow to Rosamund Grant, a tall dark woman whose strange, uncompromising beauty it would be difficult to forget. Of the Hon. Mrs Wilde he could see nothing but a pair of very large blue eyes and the tip of an abbreviated nose. The eyes gave him a brief appraising glance, and a rather high-pitched 'fashionable' voice emerged from behind the enormous fur collar:

'How do you do? Are you a relation of Charles? Too shattering for you. Charles, you will have to walk. I hate being steam-laundered even for five minutes.'

'You can sit on my knee,' said Rankin easily.

Nigel, glancing at him, noticed the peculiar bright boldness of his eyes. He was staring, not at Mrs Wilde, but at Rosamund Grant. It was as though he had said to her: 'I'm enjoying myself: I dare you to disapprove.'

She spoke for the first time, her deep voice in marked contrast to Mrs Wilde's italicized treble:

'Here comes Angela in the fire-eater,' she said, 'so there will be tons of room for everybody.'

'What a disappointment!' said Rankin. 'Marjorie, we are defeated.'

'Nothing,' said Arthur Wilde firmly, 'will persuade me to drive back in that thing with Angela.'

'Nor I neither,' agreed Rankin. 'Famous archaeologists and distinguished raconteurs should not flirt with death. Let us stay where we are.'

'Shall I wait for Miss North?' offered Nigel.

'If you would, sir,' said the chauffeur.

'Do get in, Marjorie darling,' murmured Arthur Wilde, who was sitting in the front seat. 'I'm longing for my tea and bun.'

His wife and Rosamund Grant climbed into the back of the car, and Rankin sat between them. The two-seater sports car drew up alongside.

'Sorry I'm late,' shouted Miss Angela North. 'Who's for fresh air and the open road and the wind on the heath and what-not?'

'They all sound loathsome to us,' screamed Mrs Wilde

from the Bentley. 'We are leaving you Charles's cousin.'
She opened her eyes very pointedly at Nigel. 'He's a fine,
clean-limbed young Britisher. Just your style, Angela.'
The Bentley shot away down the lane.

Feeling incapable of the correct sort of facetiousness,
Nigel turned to Angela North and uttered some
inadequate commonplace about their having met before.

'Of course we did,' she said. 'I thought you very nice.
Get in rather quickly, and let's catch them up.'

He climbed in beside her, and almost immediately had
his breath snatched away by Miss North's extremely
progressive ideas on acceleration.

'This is your first visit to Frantock,' she observed, as
they skidded dexterously round a muddy bend in the
lane. 'I hope you like it. We all think Uncle Hubert's
parties great fun . . . I don't know why, quite. Nothing
much happens at them. Everybody comes all over childish
as a rule, and silly games are played amidst loud cheers
and much laughter from those present. It's going to be
Murders this time. There they are!'

She caused the horn to give birth to a continuous belch-
ing roar, mended their speed by about fifteen or twenty
miles an hour, and passed the Bentley as it were in a
dream.

'Have you ever played Murders?' she asked.

'No, nor yet suicides, but I'm learning,' said Nigel
politely.

Angela laughed uproariously. ('She laughs like a small
boy,' thought Nigel.) 'Feeling flustered?' she shouted.
'I'm a careful driver, really.' She turned almost completely
round in her seat to wave to the receding Bentley.

'Soon be over now,' she added.

'I expect so,' breathed Nigel.

The wrought-iron posterns of a gate flashed past them,
and they dived into the rushing greyness of a wood.

'This wood's rather pleasant in the summer,' remarked

Miss North.

'It looks lovely now,' Nigel murmured, closing his eyes as they made for a narrow bridge.

A few moments later they swung into a wide curve of gravelled drive and stopped with dramatic brevity in front of a delightful old brick house.

Nigel extracted himself thankfully from the car and followed his hostess indoors.

He found himself in a really beautiful hall, dim with the smoky greyness of old oak and cheerful with the dancing comfort of a huge open fire. From the ceiling an enormous chandelier caught up the light of the flames and flickered and glowed with a strange intensity. Half drowned in the twilight that was already filling the old house, a broad staircase rose indefinitely at the far end of the hall. Nigel saw that the walls were hung conventionally with trophies and weapons . . . the insignia of the orthodox country house. He remembered Charles had told him that Sir Hubert possessed one of the finest collections of archaic weapons in England.

'If you don't mind giving yourself a drink and getting warm by the fire, I'll rouse up Uncle Hubert,' said Angela. 'Your luggage is in the other car, of course. They'll be here in a moment.'

She looked squarely at him and smiled.

'I hope I haven't completely unmanned you . . . by my driving, I mean.'

'You have . . . but not by your driving,' Nigel was astonished to hear himself reply.

'Was that gallantry? It sounded like Charles.'

Somehow he gathered that to sound like Charles was a mistake.

'I'll be back in a jiffy,' said Angela. 'There are the drinks.' She waved towards an array of glasses and disappeared into the shadows.

Nigel mixed a whisky-and-soda and wandered to the

stairs. Here he saw hanging a long strip of leather, slotted to hold a venomous company of twisted blades and tortuously wrought hafts. Nigel had stretched out his hand towards a wriggling Malay kriss, when a sudden flood of light blazed across the steel and caused him to turn abruptly. A door on his right and opened. Silhouetted against the brilliance of the room beyond was a motionless figure.

'Excuse me,' said an extremely deep voice, 'we have not met, I believe. Allow me to make an introduction of myself. Doctor Foma Tokareff. You are interested in Oriental weapons?'

Nigel had given a very noticeable start at this unexpected interruption. He recovered himself and stepped forward to meet the smiling Russian, who advanced with his hand outstretched. The young journalist closed his fist on a bunch of thin fingers that lay inert for a second and then suddenly tightened in a wiry grip. Inexplicably he felt gauche and out of place.

'I beg your pardon . . . how do you do? No . . . well, yes, interested, but I'm afraid very ill-informed,' stammered Nigel.

'Ah!' ejaculated Doctor Tokareff deeply. 'You will by compulsion learn somesing of the weapons (he pronounced it 'ooe-ponz') of the ancients if you stay here. Sir Hubert is a great authority and an enthusiastic collector.'

He spoke with extreme formality, and his phrases with their curiously stressed inflexions sounded pedantic and unreal. Nigel murmured something about being very ignorant, he was afraid, and was relieved to hear the hoot of the Bentley.

Angela came running back out of the shadows; simultaneously a butler appeared, and in a moment the hall was clamorous with the arrival of the rest of the party. A cheerful voice sounded from the head of the stairs, and Sir Hubert Handesley came down to welcome his guests.

Perhaps the secret of the success of the Frantock parties lay entirely in the charm of the host. Handesley was a singularly attractive man. Rosamund Grant once said that it wasn't fair for one individual to have so many good things. He was tall, and although over fifty years of age had retained an athlete's figure. His hair, dead white, had not suffered the indignity of middle age, but lay, thick and sleek, on his finely shaped head. His eyes were a peculiarly vivid blue, and deep-set under heavily marked brows, his lips firm and strongly compressed at the corners: altogether an almost too handsome man. His brain was of the same stereotyped quality as his looks. An able diplomat before the war, and after it a Cabinet Minister of rather orthodox brilliance, he still found time to write valuable monographs on the subject of his ruling passion —the fighting tools of the older civilizations—and to indulge his favourite hobby—he had almost made it a science—of organizing amusing house-parties.

It was characteristic of him that after a general greeting he should concentrate on Nigel, the least of his guests.

'I'm so glad you've been able to come, Bathgate,' he said. 'Angela tells me she fetched you from the station. Ghastly experience, isn't it? Charles should have warned you.'

'My dear, he was too intrepid,' shouted Mrs Wilde. 'Angela took and threw him into her squalid little tumbril, and he flashed past us with set green lips and eyes that had gazed upon stark death. Charles is so proud of his relative . . . aren't you, Charles?'

'He's a pukka sahib,' agreed Rankin solemnly.

'Are we really going to play the Murder Game?' asked Rosamund Grant. 'Angela ought to win it.'

'We are going to play A Murder Game . . . a special brand of your own, isn't it, Uncle Hubert?'

'I'll explain my plans,' said Handesley, 'when everyone has got a cocktail. People always imagine one is so much more amusing after one has given them something to drink. Will you ring for Vassily, Angela?'

'A gam' of murderings?' said Doctor Tokareff, who had been examining one of the knives. The firelight gleamed on his large spectacles, and he looked, as Mrs Wilde murmured to Rankin, 'too grimly sinister.' . . . 'A gam' of murderings? That should be sush a good fun. I am ignorant of this gam'.'

'In its cruder form it is very popular at the moment,' said Wilde, 'but I feel sure Handesley has invented subtleties that will completely transform it.'

A door on the left of the stairs opened, and through it came an elderly Slav carrying a cocktail shaker. He was greeted enthusiastically.

'Vassily Vassilyevitch,' began Mrs Wilde in Anglo-Russian of comic-opera vintage. 'Little father! Be good enough to bestow upon this unworthy hand a mouthful of your talented concoction.'

Vassily nodded his head and smiled genially. He opened the cocktail shaker, and with an air of superb and exaggerated concentration poured out a clear yellowish mixture.

'What do you think of it, Nigel?' asked Rankin. 'It's Vassily's own recipe. Marjorie calls it the Soviet Repression.'

'Not much repression about it,' murmured Arthur Wilde.

Nigel, sipping gingerly at his portion, was inclined to agree.

He watched the old Russian fussing delightedly among the guests. Angela told him that Vassily had been in her uncle's service ever since he was a young attaché at Petersburg. Nigel's eyes followed him as he moved amongst that little group of human molecules with whom, had he but known it, he himself was to become so closely and so horribly associated.

He saw his cousin, Charles Rankin, of whom, he

reflected, he knew actually so little. He sensed some sort of emotional link between Charles and Rosamund Grant. She was watching Rankin now as he leant, with something of the conventional philanderer in his pose, towards Marjorie Wilde. 'Mrs Wilde is more his affair, really, than Rosamund,' thought Nigel. 'Rosamund is too intense. Charles likes to be comfortable.' He looked at Arthur Wilde, who was talking earnestly with their host. Wilde had none of Handesley's spectacular looks, but his thin face was interesting and, to Nigel, attractive. There was quality in the form of the skull and jaw, and a sensitive elusiveness about the set of the lips.

He wondered how two such widely diverging types as this middle-aged student and his fashionable wife could ever have attracted each other. Beyond them, half in the shadow, stood the Russian doctor, his head inclined forward, his body erect and immobile.

'What does he make of us?' wondered Nigel.

'You look very grim,' said Angela at his elbow. 'Are you concocting a snappy bit for your gossip page, or thinking out a system for the Murder Game?'

Before he could answer her, Sir Hubert broke in on the general conversations: 'The dressing-bell goes in five minutes,' he said, 'so if you are all feeling strong enough, I'll explain the principles of my edition of the Murder Game.'

'Company . . . 'shun!' shouted Rankin.

CHAPTER 2

The Dagger

'The idea is this,' began Sir Hubert, as Vassily delicately circulated his mixture: 'you all know the usual version of the Murder Game. One person is chosen as the murderer, his identity being concealed from all the players. They scatter, and he seizes his moment to ring a bell or bang a gong. This symbolizes the 'murder'. They collect and hold a trial, one person being appointed as prosecuting attorney. By intensive examination he tries to discover the 'murderer'.'

'Excuse me, please,' said Doctor Tokareff. 'I am still, how you say, unintelligible. I have not been so happy to gambol in susha funny sport heretobefore, so please make him for me more clearer.'

'Isn't he sweet?' asked Mrs Wilde, a good deal too loudly.

'I will explain my version,' said Sir Hubert, 'and I think it will then be quite clear. Tonight at dinner one of us will be handed a little scarlet plaque by Vassily. I myself do not know upon which of the party his choice will fall, but let us pretend, for the sake of argument, that Mr Bathgate is cast by Vassily for the part of the murderer. He will take his scarlet plaque and say nothing to anybody. He has between five-thirty tomorrow afternoon and eleven tomorrow night as the time allotted for the performance of his "murder". He must try to get one of us alone, unknown to the others, and at the crucial moment tap him on the shoulder and say, "You are the corpse". He will then switch off the lights at the main behind the stair wall. The victim must instantly fall down as though dead, and Mr Bathgate must give one good smack at that Assyrian gong there behind the cocktail tray and make off to whatever spot he considers least incriminating. As soon as the lights go off and we hear the gong, we must all remain where we are for two minutes .. you can count your pulse-beats for a guide. At the end of two minutes we may turn up the lights. Having found the "corpse", we shall hold the trial, with the right, each of us, to cross-examine every witness. If Mr Bathgate has been clever enough, he will escape detection. I hope I have made everything reasonably understandable.'

'Pellucidly explicit,' said Doctor Tokareff. 'I shall enjoy immensely to take place in such intellectual diversion.'

'He isn't a bit pompous really,' whispered Angela in Nigel's ear, 'but he memorizes four pages of Webster's Dictionary every morning after a light breakfast. Do you hope Vassily chooses you for "murderer"?' she added aloud.

'Lord, no!' laughed Nigel. 'For one thing, I don't know the lie of the land. Couldn't you show me round the house in case I have to?'

'I will . . . tomorrow.'

'Promise?'

'Cross my heart.'

Rosamund Grant had wandered across to the foot of the stairs. She drew a long, subtly-curving dagger from the strip of leather and laid it flat upon her palm.

'The murderer has plenty of weapons to hand,' she said lightly.

'Put that beastly thing away, Rosamund,' said Marjorie Wilde, with a note of very real terror in her voice; 'they give me the horrors . . . all knives do. I can't even endure watching people carve . . . ugh!'

Rankin laughed possessively.

'I'm going to terrify you, Marjorie,' he said. 'I'm actually carrying a dagger in my overcoat pocket at this very moment.'

'Are you, Charles? But why?'

It was the first time Nigel had heard Rosamund Grant speak to his cousin that evening. She stood there on the bottom step of the stairs looking like some modern priestess of an ancient cult.

'It was sent me yesterday,' said Rankin, 'by a country-man of yours, Doctor Tokareff, whom I met in Switzerland last year. I did him rather a service—lugged him out

of a crevasse where he had lingered long enough to sacrifice
two of his fingers to frostbite — and he sent me this, as a
thank-offering, I suppose. I brought it down to show you,
Hubert . . . I thought Arthur might like to have a look at
it, too. Our famous archaeologist, you know. Let me get
it. I left my overcoat in the porch out there.'

'Vassily, get Mr Rankin's coat,' said Sir Hubert.

'I hope you don't expect me to look at it,' said Mrs
Wilde. 'I'm going to dress.'

She did not move, however, but only put her hand
through her husband's arm. He regarded her with a kind
of gentle whimsicality which Nigel thought very charming.

'It's true, isn't it, Arthur?' she said. 'I haven't read one
of your books because you will butter your pages with
native horrors.'

'Marjorie's reaction to knives or pointed tools of any
sort is not an uncommon one,' said Wilde. 'It probably
conceals a rather interesting repression.'

'Do you mean that privately she's a blood-thirster?'
asked Angela, and everyone laughed.

'Well, we shall see,' said Rankin, taking his coat from
Vassily and producing a long, carved silver case from one
of the pockets.

Nigel, who was standing beside his cousin, heard a
curiously thin, sibilant noise close behind him. He turned
his head involuntarily. At his elbow stood the old servant
transfixed, his eyes riveted on the sheath in Rankin's
hands. Instinctively Nigel glanced at Doctor Tokareff. He
too, from the farther side of the cocktail tray, was looking,
quite impassively, at the new dagger.

'By Jove!' murmured Sir Hubert quietly.

Rankin, gripping the silver sheath, slowly drew out an
excessively thin, tapering blade. He held the dagger aloft.
The blade, like a stalactite, gleamed blue in the firelight.

'It is extremely sharp,' said Rankin.

'Arthur . . . don't touch it!' cried Marjorie Wilde.

But Arthur Wilde had already taken the dagger, and was examining it under a wall-bracket lamp.

'This is quite interesting,' he murmured. 'Handesley, come and look.'

Sir Hubert joined him, and together they bent their heads over Rankin's treasure.

'Well?' asked Rankin carelessly.

'Well,' returned Wilde, 'your service to your friend, whoever he may have been, should have been of considerable value to have merited such a reward, my dear Charles. The dagger is a collector's piece. It is of extreme antiquity. Handesley and Doctor Tokareff will correct me if I am mistaken.'

Sir Hubert was staring as if, by the very intensity of his gaze, he could see back through the long perspective of its history into the mind of the craftsman who had fashioned it.

'You are right, Wilde. Of the very greatest antiquity. Obviously Mongolian. Ah, you beauty!' he whispered.

He straightened his back, and Nigel thought that he made a supreme effort to wipe away from his face and his voice all the covetousness of the ardent collector.

'Charles,' he said lightly, 'you have aroused my worst passion. How dare you!'

'What does Doctor Tokareff say?' asked Rosamund suddenly.

'I should deferentiate,' said the Russian, 'to zis august learning of Sir H. Handesley . . . and additionally to Mr Ooilde. Nevertheless, I make a suggestion that to possess zis knife is not altogezzer enviable.'

Vassily stood motionless behind Nigel. Somehow the latter was aware of his vehement concentration. Could he understand the pedantic English of his countryman?

'What do you mean?' asked Mrs Wilde sharply.

Doctor Tokareff seemed to deliberate.

'Certainly you have read,' he began at last, 'of Russian

secret brotherhoods. In my country, for many ages so unhappy, there have always been sush brotherhoods. Offten very strange, with erotic performances and mutilations . . . not so pretty, you know. In reign of Pyotr the Great, very many indeed. English shilling shockers frequently make sush silly nonsense mention. Also journalists. Excuse me, please,' to Nigel.

'Not a bit,' murmured Nigel.

'Zis knife,' continued Doctor Tokareff, 'is sacred . . . how you say? . . . symbol of one society . . . very ancient. To make presentation . . .' his voice rasped suddenly, 'was not orthodox. Therefore to personage, however noble, outside of bratsvo or brotherhood, to have zis knife is unenviable.'

Vassily surprisingly uttered a short rumbling phrase in Russian.

'This peasant agrees wis me,' said Doctor Tokareff.

'You may go, Vassily,' said Sir Hubert.

'Dressing-gong should have gone a long time ago,' said Vassily, and hurried away.

'Help!' exclaimed Angela, 'it's eight o'clock! Dinner in half an hour! Hurry, everybody.'

'Are we all in our usual rooms?' asked Mrs Wilde.

'Yes . . . oh, wait a minute . . . Mr Bathgate doesn't know. Do show him, Arthur. He's in the little Welsh room and will share your bath, my angel. Don't be late, will you, or Uncle Hubert's cook will give notice.'

'Which heaven forbid!' said Rankin fervently. 'One more . . . a very little one . . . and I'm gone.'

He poured himself out a half portion of Vassily's cock-tail, and without consulting her filled Mrs Wilde's glass again.

'Charles, you'll make me drunk,' she announced. Why does a certain type of young woman think this remark unfailingly funny? 'Don't wait for me, Arthur. I shall have Angela's bathroom when she's out of it.'

Angela and Sir Hubert had already gone. Doctor Tokareff was halfway upstairs. Arthur Wilde turned his spectacles on Nigel.

'Are you coming?'

'Yes, rather.'

Nigel followed him up the shallow staircase to a dimly lit landing.

'This is our room' explained Wilde, pointing to the first door on the left. 'The next little room I use as a dressing-room.' He opened a door farther along. 'Here you are . . . the bathroom is between us.'

Nigel found himself in a charming little oak room furnished austerely with one or two heavy old Welsh pieces. In the left wall was a door.

'This leads into our joint bathroom,' said Wilde, opening it. 'My dressing-room communicates too, you see. You go first with the bath.'

'What a jolly house it is!'

'Yes, it is extraordinarily right in every way. One grows very attached to Frantock. I expect you will find that.'

'Oh,' said the diffident Nigel. 'I don't know . . . this is my first visit . . . I may not come again.'

Wilde smiled pleasantly.

'I'm sure you will. Handesley never asks anybody unless he is sure he will want them again. I must go and help my wife find all the things she thinks her maid has forgotten. Sing out when you've finished with the bath.'

He went out through the farther door of the bathroom, and Nigel heard him humming to himself in a thin, cheerful tenor.

Finding that his very battered suitcase had already been unpacked, Nigel lost no time in bathing, shaving, and dressing. He thought of his rather grim little flatette in Ebury Street, and reflected that it would be pleasant to be able to abandon geysers and gas-rings for a cook who must not be kept waiting, and for constant hot water. In fifteen minutes he was dressed, and as he left the room could hear Wilde still splashing in the bath next door.

Nigel ran blithely downstairs, hoping that Miss Angela North had also gone down early. A door across the hall to the right of the stairs was standing open. The room beyond being brilliantly lit, he walked in and found himself alone in a big, green-panelled salon that meandered away into an L-shaped alcove, beyond which was another smaller room. This proved to be a sort of library and gun-room combined. It smelt delectably of leather bindings, gun-oil, and cigars. A bright fire was burning on the open hearth, and the gleaming barrels of Sir Hubert's sporting armoury spoke to Nigel of all the adventures he had longed for and never been able to afford.

He was gazing enviously at a Mannlicher eight when he suddenly became aware of voices in the drawing-room behind him.

It was Mrs Wilde who was speaking, and Nigel, horrified, realized that she and her companion had come in after him, had been there for some minutes, and that he had got himself into the odious position of an unwilling eavesdropper, and finally that, distasteful as this was to him, it was too late for him to announce his presence.

Hideously uncomfortable, and completely at a loss, he stood and perforce heard.

'. . . so I say you've no right to order me down like this,' she was saying in a rapid undertone. 'You treat me as if I were completely at your beck and call.'

'Well . . . don't you rather enjoy it?'

Nigel felt suddenly sick. That was Charles's voice. He heard a match scrape, and visualized his cousin's long face and sleek head slanted forward to light his cigarette. Marjorie Wilde had begun again.

'But you are insufferable, my good Charles . . .

Darling, why are you such a beast to me? You might at least—'

'Well, my dear? I might at least—what?'

'What is the position between you and Rosamund?'

'Rosamund is cryptic. She tells me she is too fond of me to marry me.'

'And yet all the time . . . with me . . . you—oh, Charles, can't you *see*?'

'Yes, I see.' Rankin's voice was furry—half tender, half possessive.

'I'm a fool,' whispered Mrs Wilde.

'Are you? Yes, you are rather a little goat. Come here.'

Her broken murmuring was suddenly checked. Silence followed, and Nigel felt positively indecent.

'Now, Madam!' said Rankin softly.

'Do you love me?'

'No. Not quite, my dear. But you're very attractive. Won't that do?'

'Do you love Rosamund?'

'Oh, good lord, Marjorie!'

'I hate you!' she said quickly. 'I could—I could . . .'

'Be quiet, Marjorie—you're making a scene. No, don't struggle. I'm going to kiss you again.'

Nigel heard a sharp, vicious little sound, rapid footsteps hurrying away, and a second later a door slammed.

'Damn!' exclaimed Charles thoughtfully. Nigel pictured him nursing his cheek. Then he, too, evidently went out by the far door. As this door opened Nigel heard voices in the hall beyond.

The booming of the gong filled the house with clamour. He went out of the gun-room into the drawing-room.

At that instant the drawing-room lights went out.

A moment later he heard the far door open and quietly close again.

Standing stock still in the abrupt darkness of this strange place, his mind worked quickly and coherently.

Marjorie Wilde and Rankin had both gone into the hall, he knew. Obviously, no one else had entered the drawing-room while they had been there. The only explanation was that someone else had been in the drawing-room hidden in the L-shaped alcove when he walked through to the gun-room, someone who, like himself, had overheard the scene between those two. His eyes soon adapted themselves to the comparative darkness. He made his way gingerly to the door, opened it, and walked out into the hall. Nobody noticed him. The entire house-party was collected round Rankin, who seemed to be concluding one of his 'pre-prandial' stories. Under cover of a roar of laughter, Nigel joined the group.

'Hullo, here he is!' exclaimed Sir Hubert. 'Everybody down? Then let's go in.'

CHAPTER 3

'You are the Corpse'

Nobody got up very early at Frantock on Sunday mornings. Nigel, wandering down to breakfast at half-past nine, found himself alone with the sausages.

He had scarcely turned his attention to the *Sunday Times* when he was told that a long-distance call had come through for him from London. He found Jamison, his taciturn chief, at the other end of the wire. 'Hullo, Bathgate. Sorry to tear you away from your champagne. How are the seats of the mighty?'

'Very much like other people's seats, only not so kick-worthy.'

'Coarse is never comic, my boy. Look here, isn't your host a bit of an authority on Russia? Well, an unknown Pole has been stuck in the gizzard in Soho, and there's some hare been started about a secret society in the West End. Sounds bogus to me, but see if you can get a story out of him. "Are Poles Russians, or are they Poles apart?" Something of that sort. Remember me to the third footman. Good morning.'

Nigel grinned and hung up the receiver. Then he paused meditatively.

'What with daggers, deaths, and eavesdroppings,' he pondered, 'there's an undercurrent of sensation in this house-party. All rather fun, but I wish old Charles wasn't cast for the first philanderer's part.'

He walked back to the dining-room. Ten minutes later he was joined by his host, who suggested a leisurely excursion through the fields.

'Arthur has a paper to write for the British Ethnological Conference, Doctor Tokareff spends his mornings in improving his vocabulary and performing other mysterious intellectual rites, Angela housekeeps, and the others are so late always that I have given up making plans for them. So if it wouldn't bore you . . .'

Nigel said eagerly that he would be anything but bored. They set out together. A thin, clear flood of wintry sunshine warmed the stark trees and rimy turf of Frantock. A sudden wave of goodwill towards anybody and everybody exhilarated Nigel. The covert ugliness of Rankin's relationship to Mrs Wilde and perhaps to Rosamund Grant was forgotten. He had been an unwilling eavesdropper—well, what of it? It could be forgotten. On an impulse he turned to his host and told him how much he was enjoying himself.

'But that is really charming of you,' said Handesley. 'I'm as susceptible as a woman to compliments about my parties. You must come again if journalism—a tiresomely exacting job, I know—will allow you the time.'

This seemed a very excellent opportunity for Nigel to get his story. He plucked up his courage and told Sir

Hubert of the telephone call from his office.

'Jamison suggested that perhaps you could give me some personal experiences of these societies—please don't if it's a nuisance—but apparently the murder of this Pole is attributed to some sort of feud in a similar organization in London.'

'I suppose it is a possibility,' said Handesley cautiously. 'But I should like to know a great deal more about the circumstances. I have written a short monograph on the Russian "brotherhoods", or rather on certain aspects of them. I'll let you have it when we go in.'

Nigel thanked him, but tentatively made the journalist's monotonous appeal for 'something a little more personal'.

'Well,' said Handesley, 'give me time, and I'll try. Why not attack Doctor Tokareff? He seems to be full of information on the subject.'

'Wouldn't he be furious? He is so very . . . is it remote?'

'And therefore beyond annoyance. He will either oblige with a sententious dissertation or refuse with a wealth of symbolism. You never know, with the Russian, whether he is really talking about the things he seems to be talking about, or whether they merely represent an abstract procession of ideas. Try him.'

'I will,' said Nigel, and they finished their walk in companionable silence.

Looking back on the Frantock affair after it was all over, Nigel always thought of that walk as the one perfect and peaceful episode during his visit. At luncheon he was aware once more of the secondary theme of dissonance between Rankin, Rosamund, and Mrs Wilde. He suspected, too, an antagonism between Tokareff and Rankin and, being particularly sensitive to the timbre of emotional relationships, was mentally on tenterhooks.

After luncheon they all went their ways—Handesley and Tokareff to the library, Mrs Wilde and Rankin for a stroll, Nigel and Angela to explore the house (with a view to the former learning his way about it for the Murder Game), and then to play badminton in the barn. Rosamund Grant and Wilde had disappeared, whether severally or together Nigel had no idea. He and Angela got extremely hot, laughed a great deal and, each delighted with the other's company, arrived back in the hall in time for tea.

'Now,' said Handesley, when Angela had poured out the last cup, 'it's twenty-five minutes past five. At half-past the Murder Game is on. By eleven it must be an accomplished fact. You all know the rules. Last night Vassily gave the scarlet plaque to whichever one of us he selected as murderer. I remind you that the "murderer" is to turn out the lights and sound the gong, that you are not by word or look to suggest that you have been discarded or selected by Vassily as actor for the part of assassin. The "murderer" has had a day in which to formulate his plans. There—that's all.'

'Okay, chief,' drawled Rankin.

'Meet me behind the arras, be your purpose bloody,' said Wilde sweetly.

'Any questions?' asked Handesley.

'Sush admirable terse discourse makes no jot of confusion. Already I am, as you say, on tendercooks,' murmured Doctor Tokareff.

'Well,' concluded Handesley cheerfully, 'let us wish the murderer at any rate an interesting amount of success.'

'I'm not sure.' said Mrs Wilde, 'that this game isn't going to be rather terrifying.'

'I call it a definite thrill,' remarked Angela.

Sir Hubert walked over to the gong and took the leather-padded hammer in his hand. They all watched the grandfather clock that stood in the farthest corner of the hall. The long hand jerked across the last division, and

the clock, deep voiced, told the half-hour. At the same
moment Handesley struck the gong.

'Murder is afoot,' he said theatrically; 'the gong shall
not sound again until it is accomplished . . . Shall we
move into the drawing-room?'

Nigel, thankful that Vassily's choice had not fallen
upon himself, speculated on the possible identity of the
'murderer', determined to make a mental note of everybody's movements, and equally to be left alone with no
single member of the house-party, since he felt that the
role of 'corpse' would be less amusing than that of witness
or Prosecuting Attorney.

In the drawing-room Mrs Wilde started a rag by
suddenly hurling a cushion at—of all people—Doctor
Tokareff. To the astonishment and discomfiture of everybody, the Russian, after a brief moment of blank bewil-
derment, suddenly developed a species of mad playfulness.
Always, to English people, there is something rather
embarrassing about a foreigner playing the fool. Doctor
Tokareff, however, was quite unaware of this racial self-
consciousness.

'Is not this,' he exclaimed joyously, 'indication of
British tatter or scrap? I am reading that when English
lady propels cush at head of gentleman, she connotes
sporting desire.' And with that he hurled the cushion at
Mrs Wilde with such accuracy and force that she
completely lost her balance and fell into Rankin's arms.
With one hand he held her closely against him and with
the other whirled the cushion about his head, striking the
Russian full in the face.

For a second Nigel saw that Doctor Tokareff's face was
capable of expressing something divorced from tranquil
amiability.

'Look out!' he shouted involuntarily.

But the doctor had stepped back with a little bow and
was smiling holding up his hands. There was an un-

comfortable silence.

'I'm on Doctor Tokareff's side,' said Angela suddenly, and collared Rankin about the knees.

'So am I,' said Rosamund. 'Charles, do you like your face rubbed up or down?'

'Let's de-bag old Arthur,' suggested Rankin, emerging breathless from the hurly-burly. 'Come on, Nigel . . . come on, Hubert.'

'There's always something wrong with old Charles when he rags,' thought Nigel. But he held the protesting Wilde while his trousers were dragged off, and joined in the laugh when he stood pale and uncomfortable, clutching a hearth-rug to his recreant limbs and blinking short-sightedly.

'You've smashed my spectacles,' he said.

'Darling!' screamed Mrs Wilde, 'you look too stupid to be believed. Charles, what a horror you are to make such nonsense of my husband!'

'I feel I look rather magnificent,' declared Wilde. 'Who's got my trousers? You, Angela! My Edwardian blood congeals at the sight. Give them up, child, or I grow churlish.'

'Here you are, Adonis,' said Rankin, snatching the trousers from Angela and tying them round Wilde's neck. 'Gosh, what a lovely sight! Perfect picture of a gentleman who has stroked his eight to victory.'

'Run and put them on, my pet,' said Mrs Wilde, 'or you'll get growing pains.'

Wilde obediently disappeared.

'Last time I de-bagged Arthur was at Eton,' said Rankin. 'God, what ages ago it seems!'

He turned to the wireless and began tuning in to a concert of dance music.

'Come on, Rosamund,' he said, 'let's dance.'

'I'm too hot,' said Rosamund, who had been talking to Tokareff.

'Marjorie!' shouted Rankin, 'can you bear to trip a measure?'

'Has Rosamund turned you down? Too dreary for you, Charles.'

'I've let him off his duty dance,' said Rosamund. 'Doctor Tokareff is telling a story a thousand years old, and I must hear the end.'

'This is a history,' began Tokareff, 'of a hospodin . . . a noble . . . and two ladies. It is what you call eternal triangle . . . very old motif in human history.'

'So old that it is, don't you think, rather boring?' asked Rankin.

'Do dance, Marjorie,' said Angela.

Without waiting for her consent, Rankin put his arm round Mrs Wilde, and at once Nigel saw that she was translated.

There are some women who, when they dance, express a depth of feeling and of temperament that actually they do not possess. He saw that Mrs Wilde was one of these women. Under the spell of that blatantly exotic measure she seemed to flower, to become significant and dangerous. Rankin, rapt and serious, was at once her foil and her master. He never took his eyes off hers, and she, unfriendly, provocative, stared back at him as though she were insulting him. Nigel, Angela, and Handesley stopped talking to watch these two, and Wilde, returning, stood stock still in the doorway. Only the Russian seemed disinterested. He had bent over the wireless set and was examining it intently.

The quicker second movement slid back into the original theme of the tango. The dancers had come together in the first steps of their final embrace, when an ear-splitting shriek from the wireless shattered the spell.

'What the devil!' exclaimed Rankin angrily.

'Please forgive,' said Tokareff calmly. 'Evidently I have blundered. Sush a funny muck-up and screechiness

I never before have heard . . .'

'Wait a moment . . . I'll get it back,' suggested Handesley.

'No, no, don't bother—it would be too stupid to go on,' answered Rankin ungraciously. He lit a cigarette and walked away from his partner.

'Charles,' said Handesley quietly, 'Arthur and I have been discussing your dagger. It really is enormously interesting. Do be a little more forthcoming about its history.'

'All I can tell you,' said Rankin, 'is this. I pulled a wild-looking gentleman out of a crevasse in Switzerland last year. I don't speak Russian, and he didn't speak English. I never saw him again, but apparently he traced me—through my guide, I suppose—to my hotel, and thence, presumably, to England. The knife with the two words, "Switzerland" (so lavish) and "thanks" only reached me yesterday. I conclude it was from him.'

'Will you sell it to me, Charles?' asked Sir Hubert. 'I'll give you much more than you deserve for it.'

'No, Hubert, I won't. But I'll tell you what I will do. I'll leave it to you. Nigel here gets all my possessions. Nigel! If I kick the bucket, my lad, Hubert is to have the dagger. Bear witness, all of you.'

'It shall be done,' said Nigel.

'Considering I'm ten years your senior, it's not what I should call a handsome offer,' complained Handesley. 'Still, let's have it in writing.'

'You old ghoul, Hubert!' laughed Rankin.

'Hubert!' shrieked Marjorie Wilde, 'how can you be so utterly bloodsucking!'

Rankin had walked to the writing-desk.

'Here you are, you maniac,' he said. 'Nigel and Arthur can witness.'

He wrote the necessary phrase and signed it. Nigel and Wilde witnessed, and Rankin handed it to Handesley.

'You'd much better sell it to me,' said Handesley coolly.

'Excuse me, please,' boomed Doctor Tokareff. 'I do not entirely understand.'

'No?' The note of antagonism had crept into Rankin's voice. 'I merely leave instructions that if a sticky end should overtake me—'

'Excuse me, please . . . a sticky end?'

'Oh, damn! If I should die, or be murdered, or disappear from view, this knife which you, Doctor Tokareff, consider has no business to be in my possession, shall become the property of our host.'

'Thank you,' said Doctor Tokareff composedly.

'You do not approve?'

'*Niet*. No. By my standpoint of view, zis knoife does not belong by you.'

'The knife was given to me.'

'Such indiscretion has doubtless been suitably chastized,' remarked the Russian peacefully.

'Well,' broke in Handesley, noting perhaps the two little scarlet danger signals in Rankin's cheeks, 'let us hope it will give no offence by hanging for tonight at the foot of my stairs. Come and have a cocktail.'

Charles Rankin lingered in the drawing-room with his cousin. He slipped his arm through Nigel's.

'Not a very delicious gentleman, that dago,' he said loudly.

'Look out, he'll hear you!'

'I don't give a damn.'

Wilde paused in the doorway and detained them.

'I shouldn't let it worry you, Charles,' he said in his diffident voice. 'His point of view is not unreasonable. I know something of these societies.'

'Oh, hell, what's it matter, anyway? Come and let's drink. This murder's got to be done.'

Nigel glanced at him sharply.

'No, no,' laughed Rankin, 'not by me . . . I didn't mean that. By someone.'

'I'm not going to be left alone with anyone,' Mrs Wilde was announcing.

'I wonder,' speculated Handesley, 'if that's true — or is it a bluff? Or am I bluffing?'

'I'm going to take my drink up with me,' said Rosamund. 'No one will try to murder me in my bath, I hope, and I shan't come down till I hear voices in the hall.'

'I'll come up with you, Rosamund,' said Mrs Wilde and Angela simultaneously.

'I also will make myself for the dining,' announced Doctor Tokareff.

'Wait a bit!' called Handesley. 'I'm coming up. I won't go down that passage alone!'

There was a concerted stampede upstairs, only Nigel, Rankin, and Wilde being left in the hall.

'Shall I bath first,' Nigel asked Wilde.

'Yes, do,' he agreed. 'It's safe enough for Charles and me to be left together. Whichever of us tries to do in the other would be accused by you as the last person to see the corpse alive. I claim the bath in ten minutes.'

Nigel ran upstairs, leaving the two men to finish their drinks. He bathed quickly and dressed at leisure. The Murder Game was distinctly amusing. For some reason he rather thought that Vassily had given the scarlet plaque to his compatriot. Nigel determined not to go down until he heard Doctor Tokareff's voice. 'After all,' he thought, 'it would be easy enough for him to catch me as I opened my door and then go downstairs as if nothing had happened, choose his moment to put out the lights, sound the gong, and then move away in the darkness and stand still for the two minutes, asking at the top of his voice who had done it. That wouldn't be a bad plan of action, by Jove.'

He heard the bathroom door open. A moment later the taps were turned on, and Wilde's voice called out to him:

'No bloodshed yet, Bathgate?'

'Not yet,' shouted Nigel. 'But I'm much too frightened to go down.'

'Let's wait till Marjorie is ready,' suggested Wilde, 'and all go down together. If you don't agree, I'll know you are the murderer.'

'All right, I'll agree,' yelled Nigel cheerfully, and he heard Wilde laugh to himself and shout the suggestion through to his wife, who was presumably still dressing in the room beyond.

Nigel walked over to his bedside table and picked up the book he had been reading the night before. It was Joseph Conrad's *Suspense*. He had just opened it at the title-page when there was a light tap on the door.

'Come in,' shouted Nigel.

A rather flustered and extremely pretty housemaid appeared.

'Oh, please, sir,' she began, 'I'm afraid I've forgot your shaving-water.'

'It's all right,' said Nigel. 'I managed with—' Suddenly the room was completely blacked out.

He stood in thick darkness with the invisible book in his hand while the voice of the gong—primitive and threatening—surged up through the empty throat of the house. It filled the room with an intolerable clamour and then died away grudgingly. Silence flowed back again and, trickling through it, the noise of the bath-water still running next door. Then Wilde's voice shouting excitedly:

'I say . . . what's all this—?'

'Pretty nippy, wasn't it?' shouted Nigel. 'What about the two minutes? Wait a bit. I've got a luminous wrist watch. I'll keep time for both of us.'

'Yes, but look here—do I have to lie in this bath,' queried Wilde plaintively, 'or do you imagine I may get out and dry myself?'

'Pull out the plug and reach for the towel. Did you leave Charles downstairs?'

'Yes, I did. Full of complaints about Tokareff. I say, do you think . . .' Wilde's voice became muffled. Evidently he had found the towel.

'Time!' said Nigel. 'I'm off.'

'Turn up the lights, for heaven's sake,' urged Wilde. 'I'm going to miss all the fun if I can't find my pants.'

His wife's voice screeched excitedly from the far room. 'Arthur, wait for me!'

'Me wait for you—' began Wilde in an injured voice.

Nigel struck a match and made his way to the door. Out on the landing it was pitch dark, but farther back along the passage he could see little points of matchlight and the dramatic uncertainty of faces, dimly lit from below. Far down beneath him in the hall was the comfortable flicker of a fire. The house was alive with the voices of the guests, calling, laughing, questioning. Cosseting his match, he groped his way downstairs; it burnt out, but the firelight enabled him to round the bottom of the stairs and find the main switch.

For a second he hesitated. Obscurely, unaccountably, he did not want to wipe away the darkness. As he stood with his hand on the switch, time seemed to hang still.

From the stairs Handesley's voice called out:

'Anyone find the switch?'

'I'm there,' answered Nigel, and his hand jerked it down.

The sudden blaze from the chandelier was blinding. On the stairs Wilde, his wife, Tokareff, Handesley, and Angela all shrank back from it. Nigel, blinking, came round the stairs. Facing him was the cocktail tray, and beside him the great Assyrian gong.

A man was lying on his face alongside the table. He was lying at right angles to the gong.

Nigel, still blinking, turned his face towards the others. 'I say,' he said, peering at them and shading his eyes. 'I say, look . . . here he is.'

'It's Charles,' exclaimed Mrs Wilde shrilly.

'Poor old Charles!' said Handesley jovially.

They were all pushing and shouting. Only Rankin did not move.

'Don't touch him . . . don't touch him, anybody,' said Angela; 'you must never disturb the body, you know.'

'A moment, please.' Doctor Tokareff put her gently aside. He came downstairs, glanced at Nigel, who stood transfixed, staring at his cousin, and bent down slowly.

'This young lady speaks with wisdom,' said Doctor Tokareff. 'Undoubtedly, let us not touch.'

'Charles,' screamed Mrs Wilde suddenly. 'My God, Charles! . . . Charles!'

But Rankin lay heavily silent and, their eyes having grown accustomed to the light, they all saw the hilt of his Russian dagger jutting out like a little horn between his shoulder-blades.

CHAPTER 4

Monday

Chief Detective-Inspector Alleyn was accosted by Detective-Inspector Boys in the corridor outside his office.

'What's the matter with you?' said Inspector Boys. 'Has someone found you a job?'

'You've guessed my boyish secret. I've been given a murder to solve — aren't I a lucky little detective?'

He hurried out into the main corridor, where he was met by Detective-Sergeant Bailey who carried a finger-print apparatus, and by Detective-Sergeant Smith who was burdened with a camera. A car was waiting for them, and in two hours' time they were standing in the hall at Frantock.

PC Bunce of the local constabulary eyed the inspector cautiously.

'A very nasty business, sir,' he said with relish. 'The superintendent being took very bad with the 'flu and no one else here to handle the case except the sergeant, we rang up the Yard immediately. This is Doctor Young, the divisional surgeon who made the examination.' A sandy-coloured, palish man had stepped forward.

'Good morning,' said Inspector Alleyn. 'No doubt about the medical verdict, I suppose?'

'None whatever, I'm grieved to say,' said the doctor, whose accent had a smack of Scots in it. 'I was called in immediately after the discovery. Life had been extinct about thirty minutes. There is no possibility of the injury being self-inflicted. The superintendent here has an acute attack of gastric influenza and is really quite unfit to do anything. I gave definite instructions that he was not to be worried about the case. In view of the most extraordinary circumstances and also of Sir Hubert's position, the local office decided to approach Scotland Yard.' Doctor Young stopped talking suddenly as if someone had turned his voice off at the main. He then made a deep, uncomfortable noise in his throat, a noise that sounded like 'Kaahoom'.

'The body?' queried Inspector Alleyn.

The constable and the doctor began to speak together.

'Beg parding, doctor,' said PC Bunce.

'It has been moved into the study,' explained the doctor; 'it had already been greatly disturbed. I could see no point in leaving it here — in the hall — very difficult.'

'Greatly disturbed? By whom? But let me have the whole story. Shall we sit down, Doctor Young? I really know nothing of the case.'

They sat down before the great fireplace, where only

twelve hours ago Rankin had warmed himself as he told one of his 'pre-prandial' stories.

'The victim's name,' began Doctor Young in a businesslike voice, 'was Rankin. He was one of a party of five guests spending the weekend with Sir Hubert Handesley and his niece. They had been playing one of these new-fangled games, one called—' he paused for a second—'called "Murders". You may have heard of it.'

'Don't play it myself,' said Inspector Alleyn. 'I'm not frightfully keen on busman's holidays. But I think I know what you mean. Well?'

'Well, I gather they were all dressing for dinner—you will hear all the details from the guests, of course—when the signal agreed upon was sounded, and on coming down they found not a sham but a real victim.'

'Where was he lying?'

'Over here.' The doctor crossed the hall, and Inspector Alleyn followed him. The floor in front of the gong had been newly washed and smelt of disinfectant.

'On his face?'

'In the first instance, yes, but as I say, the body had been moved. A dagger, Russo-Chinese and his own property, had been driven in between the shoulders at such an angle that it had pierced the heart. Instantaneous.'

'I see. It's no good my making a song and dance about the moving of the body and washing the floor—now. The damage is done. You should never have allowed it, Doctor Young. Never, no matter how much the original position had been lost.'

Doctor Young looked extremely uncomfortable.

'I am very sorry. Sir Hubert was most anxious—it was, it *was* very difficult. The body had been moved some considerable distance.'

'Do you think I could have a word with Sir Hubert,' asked Alleyn—'before we go any further, I mean?'

'I am sure you can presently. He is very much shocked, of course, and I have suggested his trying to rest for a couple of hours. His niece, Miss Angela North, is expecting you, and is to let him know of your arrival. I'll just find her.'

'Thank you. By the way, where are the rest of the house-party?'

'They've bin warned not to leave the house,' said Mr Bunce capably, 'and in addition they bin kept away from the hall and the drawing-room and asked particular to only frequent the library. Except for the floor being cleaned up nothing here's bin touched, sir, nothing. And the drawing-room's left just as it was too — just in case.'

'Excellent; aren't our policemen wonderful? And so they are — where?'

'One of the ladies is in bed and the rest of the bunch is in the librar-rary,' he jerked his thumb over his shoulder, 'a-solving of the mystery.'

'That should prove very interesting,' said the inspector without any taint of irony in his pleasant voice. 'If you would get Miss North, Doctor Young.'

The doctor hurried upstairs and the Law was left in possession.

Inspector Alleyn held a brief colloquy with his two subordinates.

'If there has really been no interference, there ought to be something for you here, Bailey,' he said to the finger-print expert. 'From information received we'll want prints of the entire household. While I am seeing the people, get busy in here. And you, Sergeant Smith, get me a picture of the area where the body was found, and of course a photo of the body itself.'

'Certainly, sir.'

PC Bunce listened appreciatively.

'Ever had any dealings with a case of this sort before, constable?' asked the inspector absent-mindedly.

'Never, sir. Petty larceny's the best they can do in these parts, with a smack of furious driving, and one haryplane smash three years ago. Bit of an ad. for the village if looked on in the right light. We've got a special reporter on the spot, too.'

'Really! How do you mean?'

'A Mr Bathgate, sir, of the *Clarion*. He's staying here, sir.'

'Singularly fortunate,' said Inspector Alleyn drily.

'Yes, sir. Here he is, sir.'

Angela came downstairs with the doctor and with Nigel. She was extremely white and had about her the pathetic dignity of the very young when they meet disaster with fortitude. Inspector Alleyn met her at the foot of the stairs.

'I'm so sorry to have to bother you like this,' he said, 'but I understand from Doctor Young . . .'

'Not a bit,' said Angela. 'We were expecting you. This is Mr Bathgate, who has been very kind about telegraphing and helping us. He is—he is Mr Rankin's cousin.'

Nigel shook hands. Since he had seen Charles lying—empty, unmeaning, coldly remote—at his feet, he could feel neither sorrow nor horror—not even pity; and yet he supposed he had been fond of Charles.

'I'm very sorry,' said Inspector Alleyn; 'this must have been distressing for you. May we go and talk somewhere?'

'There's no one in the drawing-room,' said Angela. 'Shall we go in there?'

They sat in the drawing-room where Charles Rankin had danced a tango with Mrs Wilde the previous afternoon. Between them Angela and Nigel recounted to the inspector the history of the Murder Game.

Angela had time for a good long stare at her first detective. Alleyn did not resemble a plain-clothes policeman, she felt sure, nor was he in the romantic manner—white faced and gimlet eyed. He looked like one of her Uncle Hubert's friends, the sort that they knew would 'do' for house-parties. He was very tall, and lean, his hair was dark, and his eyes grey, with corners that turned down. They looked as if they would smile easily, but his mouth didn't. 'His hands and his voice are grand,' thought Angela, and subconsciously she felt less miserable.

Angela told Nigel afterwards that she approved of Inspector Alleyn. He treated her with a complete absence of any show of personal interest, an attitude that might have piqued this modern young woman under less tragic circumstances. As it was, she was glad of his detachment. Little Doctor Young sat and listened, repeating every now and then his inarticulate, consolatory noise. Alleyn made a few notes in his pocket-book.

'The parlour-game, you say,' he murmured, 'was limited to five and a half hours — that is to say, it began at five-thirty, and should have ended before eleven — ended with the mock trial. The body was found at six minutes to eight. Doctor Young arrived some thirty minutes later. Just let me get that clear — I've a filthy memory.'

At this unorthodox and slightly unconvincing statement Doctor Young and Angela started.

'And now, if you please,' said the inspector, 'I should like to see the other members of the household — one by one, you know. In the meantime Doctor Young can take me into the study. Perhaps you and Miss North will find out if Sir Hubert is feeling up to seeing me.'

'Certainly,' agreed Angela. She turned to Nigel. 'Afterwards, will you wait for me?'

'I'll wait for you, Angela,' said Nigel.

In the study Inspector Alleyn bent over the silent heaviness of Rankin's body. He stared at it for a full two minutes, his lips closed tightly and a sort of fastidiousness wringing the corners of his mouth, his nostrils, and his eyes. Then he stooped, and turning the body on to its side, closely examined, without touching, the dagger that had been left there, still eloquent of the gesture that had driven it through Rankin's bone and muscle into the citadel of his heart.

'You can be no end of a help to me here,' said Alleyn. 'The blow, of course, came from above. Looks beastly, doesn't it? The point entered the body as you see — here. Surely something of an expert's job.'

The little doctor, who had been greatly chastened by the official rebuke on the subject of the removal of the body, leapt at the chance of re-establishing himself.

'Great force and, I should have thought, a considerable knowledge of anatomy are indicated. The blade entered the body to the right of the left scapula and between the third and fourth ribs, avoiding the spine and the vertebral border of the scapula. It lies at an acute angle and the point has penetrated the heart.'

'Yes, I rather imagined it had done that,' said Alleyn sweetly, 'but mightn't this have been due to — shall we say luck, possibly?'

'Possibly,' said the doctor stiffly. 'I think not!'

The faintest hint of a smile crept into Alleyn's eyes.

'Come on, Doctor Young,' he said quietly, 'you've got your own ideas, I see. What are they?'

The little doctor looked down his little nose and a glint of mild defiance hardened his uneventful face.

'I realize, of course, that under such very grave circumstances one should put a guard upon one's tongue,' he said, 'nevertheless, perhaps in camera, as it were . . .'

'Every detective,' remarked Alleyn, 'has to acquire something of the attitude of the priest. "In camera" let it be, Doctor Young.'

'I have only this to say. Before I arrived last night the body had been turned over and — and — gone over by a Russian gentleman who appears to be a medico. This in spite of the fact —' here Doctor Young's accent became more definitely Northern — 'that I was summoned immediately after the discovery. Possibly in Soviet Russia the finer shades of professional etiquette are not considered.'

Inspector Alleyn looked at him. 'A considerable knowledge of anatomy, you said,' he murmured vaguely. 'Ah, well, we shall see what we shall see. How extraordinary it is,' he went on, gently laying Rankin down; 'his face is quite inscrutable. If only something could be written there. I should like to see Sir Hubert now if that is possible.'

'I will ascertain,' said Doctor Young formally, and left Rankin and Alleyn alone in the study.

Handesley was already waiting in the hall. Nigel and Angela were with him. Nigel was perhaps more shocked by the change in his host and more alive to it than to anything else that had happened since Rankin's death. Handesley looked ghastly. His hands were tremulous and he moved with a kind of controlled hesitancy.

Alleyn came into the hall and was formally introduced by little Doctor Young, who seemed to be somewhat nonplussed by the inspector's markedly Oxonian voice.

'I am sorry to have kept you waiting,' said Handesley. 'I am quite ready to answer any questions that you would like to put to me.'

'There are very few at the moment,' returned Alleyn. 'Miss North and Mr Bathgate have given me a clear account of what happened since yesterday afternoon. Could we, do you think, go into some other room?'

'The drawing-room is just here,' answered Handesley. 'Do you wish to see us there in turn?'

'That will do splendidly,' agreed Alleyn.

'The others are in the library,' said Nigel. Handesley turned to the detective. 'Then shall we go into the drawing-room?'

'I think I can ask you the few questions I want to put immediately. The others can come in there afterwards. I understand, Sir Hubert, that Mr Rankin was an old friend of yours?'

'I have known him all his life—I simply cannot take it in—this appalling tragedy. It is incredible. We—we all knew him so well. It must have been someone from outside. It must.'

'How many servants do you keep? I should like to see them later on. But in the meantime if I may have their names.'

'Yes, of course. It is imperative that everyone should—should be able to give an account of himself. But my servants! I have had them for years, all of them. I can think of no possible motive.'

'The motive is not going to be one of the kind that socks you on the jaw. If I may have a list.'

'My butler is a Little Russian. He was my servant twenty years ago in Petersburg, and has been with me ever since.'

'He was well acquainted with Mr Rankin?'

'Very well acquainted. Rankin has stayed here regularly for many years and has always been on excellent terms with my servants.'

'They tell me the dagger is of Russian origin.'

'Its history is Russian, its origin Mongolian,' said Sir Hubert. He briefly related the story of the knife.

'H'm,' said Alleyn. 'Scratch a Russian and you use a Mongolian knife. Had your servant seen this delightful museum piece?'

'Yes. He must have seen it. Now I come to think of it, he was in the hall when Rankin first produced it.'

'Did he comment on it in any way?'

'Vassily? No,' Handesley hesitated and turned to Nigel and Angela. 'Wait a moment, though. Didn't he say something when Tokareff was holding forth about the knife and its association with a bratsvo?'

'I think he did,' said Nigel slowly. 'He made some remark in Russian. Doctor Tokareff said, "This peasant agrees with me," and you, sir, told Vassily he could go.'

'That is how it was,' agreed Angela.

'I see. Rum coincidence that the knife, your butler, and your guest should all be of the same nationality.'

'Not very odd,' said Angela. 'Uncle Hubert has always kept up his interest in Russia—especially since the war. Charles was familiar with his collection of weapons and brought this horrible thing down specially for Uncle Hubert to see.'

'Yes. Is the dagger interesting from the point of view of the collector?'

Handesley winced and glanced at Angela. 'It interested me enormously,' he said. 'I offered to buy it.'

'Really? Did Mr Rankin want to sell?'

There was a very uncomfortable pause. Nigel miserably cast about in his mind for something to say. Suddenly Angela broke the silence.

'You are very tired, Uncle Hubert,' she said gently; 'let me tell Mr Alleyn.' Without waiting for his reply, she turned to the detective.

'Charles Rankin, in fun, wrote out a statement last night willing the knife to my uncle. Mr Bathgate here and Mr Arthur Wilde, another of our guests, signed the paper. It was all a joke.'

Alleyn, without any comment, made a note in his pocket-book. 'Perhaps I may see this paper later on,' he said; 'and now for the other servants.'

'All English,' said Angela, 'except the cook, who is a Frenchman. There are three maids, two housemaids, and a little Cockney—she's a tweeney really—a sort of pantryman who, when we have large parties, does footman and helps Vassily, a kitchenmaid, and an odd-boy.'

'Thank you. Mr Bathgate, you, I understand, are Mr Rankin's cousin. To your knowledge, had he any enemies? This, I know, sounds a childish inquiry, but I think I shall put it to you.'

'To *my* knowledge,' answered Nigel, 'none. Obviously he had one.'

'Nobody who would benefit by his death?'

'Benefit?' Nigel's voice grated suddenly. 'My God, yes. I benefit. I believe he has left me the bulk of his property. You'd better arrest me, Inspector—I killed him for his money.'

'My good young man,' said Alleyn tartly, 'please don't muddle me with startling announcements of that sort. It is incredibly silly. Here are two witnesses to your theatricality. Pull yourself together and leave me to do my detecting. It's tricky enough as it is, lord knows.'

The unexpectedness of this rebuke had a very salutary effect on Nigel. For a second it lifted him out of his nightmare of shocked reactions.

'Sorry,' he said. 'I don't really want to leap into the handcuffs.'

'So I should hope. Now run off and find the assembled guests. I think, the local bluebottle buzzed something about the library. Send them along singly to the drawing-room; and, Miss North, will you find the servants?'

'Mrs Wilde,' said Angela, 'was in bed a little while ago. She is terribly upset.'

'I am sorry, but I should like everyone to be present.'

'Very well, I'll tell her.' Angela went upstairs.

Having started off the examination with Arthur Wilde, Nigel waited with Sir Hubert in the garden. Apparently the detective spent a very short time over his interviews, for Nigel had smoked only two cigarettes when Mr Bunce emerged with the tidings that the chief inspector was at Sir Hubert's service. They went indoors and joined Alleyn. Handesley led the way down the hall, where Mr Bunce still kept guard, into the big library that lay behind the drawing-room and the little gun-room. At the door he paused and looked intently at the inspector.

'I see from your card,' he said courteously, 'that your

name is Roderick Alleyn. I was up at Oxford with a very brilliant man of that name. A relation, perhaps?'

'Perhaps,' said the inspector politely but uncommunicatively. He stepped back to allow Nigel to open the library door, and they went in. Here all the others, with the exception of Marjorie Wilde, were already assembled. Tokareff's voice could be heard booming as the door opened, and on their entrance they found him standing before the fire, bespectacled, earnest, and resoundingly verbose. Rosamund Grant, deadly white, was sitting in a far corner of the room, immaculate and withdrawn. Arthur Wilde, with an air of strained attention, appeared to be listening, dubiously, to the Russian's dissertation. Doctor Young was fidgeting in the bow-window.

'. . . so to take a loife from my standpoint-of-view is not such a crime as to be always living a false loife,' shouted Tokareff. 'Zhis is the real crime more deadly—' He stopped suddenly as Handesley and Alleyn, followed by Nigel and Angela, came towards him.

'Inspector Alleyn,' said Handesley briefly, 'wishes to speak to us all for a moment.'

'Already,' began Tokareff, 'we have been interviewed. Already the hunt is to begin. Excuse me, please, but I must make myself clear to say—'

'Will you all please sit round this table?' said Alleyn, incisively cutting through the clamour of Tokareff's rumbling bass.

They all moved across to a long writing-table near the windows and seated themselves at it, Alleyn taking the head.

'I have only this to say,' he said quietly. 'A man was done to death in this house at five minutes to eight last night. It is possible—but only just possible—that the crime was brought off by someone from the outside. Until the inquest is over I'm afraid no one may leave Frantock. You will all, if you please, confine yourselves to the house and grounds. Should any of you want to go farther afield, just let me know, will you? And if the reason is urgent, I'll provide a suitable.escort. You will be at liberty to use the hall and drawing-room an hour after this little chat is ended. During that hour I must ask you to allow me to make my examination of those rooms.'

There was a difficult silence. Then Rosamund Grant spoke.

'For how long will these restrictions be enforced?' she asked. Her voice, level and expressionless, suddenly and shockingly reminded Nigel of Rankin's.

'The inquest will probably be held on Thursday,' said Alleyn. 'Until after then, at all events, I shall ask you to stay where you are.'

'Is this absolutely necessary?' asked Handesley. 'I am of course, only too anxious for every effort to be made, but I understand some of my guests — Mrs Wilde, for instance — are naturally longing to get away from the unhappy associations of my house.' A foreign overtone of deprecation in his voice filled Nigel suddenly with an enormous sense of pity.

'Sir Hubert,' he said quickly, 'the situation is more difficult for you than for any of us. If we must stay, we must, but I am sure we will, all of us, try to be as little nuisance and as much help as may be. Under such circumstances all personal considerations must go to blazes. I'm afraid that's not very well put, but—'

'I entirely agree,' broke in Wilde. 'It is inconvenient, but convenience hardly counts at such a time. My wife, I am sure, will understand this.'

As if in answer to this assertion the door was opened and Marjorie Wilde came in.

The placing of the others, the tenseness of the moment and the lateness of her arrival gave it something of the character of a theatrical entrance. There was, however, little else that was stagey about Mrs Wilde's appearance.

She came in very quietly, her make-up was much less vigorously stated than usual and her clothes, as Nigel found himself reflecting, contrived to look like mourning.

'I'm very sorry to have kept you all waiting,' she murmured. 'Please don't move, anyone.'

Her husband pulled a chair up for her, and at last they were all seated at the table.

'Now,' said Alleyn, 'I understand, I think, the general principles and the history of this game which ended so strangely and so tragically. I do not, however, quite realize what would have happened if a sham instead of a real victim had been found—'

'But excuse me,' began Tokareff, 'is this, how you say, a relevancy?'

'It is quite in order, otherwise I should not ask. What would you have done in the ordinary course of the game?' He turned to Wilde.

'We should,' said Wilde, 'have immediately assembled and held a mock trial, with a "judge" and a "prosecuting attorney", each of us having the right to cross-examine. Our object would have been to find the "murderer"— the member of the party to whom Vassily had given the scarlet plaque.'

'Thank you—yes, I see. And you have not done this?'

'Good God, Inspector,' said Nigel violently. 'What do you take us for?'

'He takes one of us for a criminal,' said Rosamund slowly.

'I think the Murder Game should be played out,' Alleyn continued. 'I propose that we hold the trial precisely as it was planned. I shall play the part of prosecuting attorney. I'm not very good at official language, but I'll do my poor best. For the moment there will be no judge. That will be the only difference between this and the original version—except that I hope there will be no difficulty in at once discovering the recipient of the scarlet plaque.'

'There will be no difficulty,' said Wilde. 'Vassily gave the scarlet plaque to me.'

CHAPTER 5

Mock Trial

Arthur Wilde's announcement had a dramatic effect quite out of proportion to its real value. Nigel experienced a violent emotional shock, followed immediately by the reflection that, after all, the identity of the recipient of the plaque had very little bearing on the case.

It was odd that they should none of them have thought of locating the 'villain' in the game. That was all.

Complete silence followed Wilde's statement. Rosamund broke it. 'Oh well,' she said evenly, 'what of that?'

'Thank you very much, Mr Wilde,' said Alleyn. The inspector's manner had undoubtedly become most convincingly official. 'You have come forward as the first witness. You were given the plaque at dinner?'

'Yes—Vassily slipped it into my hand as I helped myself to the savoury.'

'Had you formed any definite plan about carrying out your role in the game?'

'Not precisely. I was thinking it over as I lay in my bath. Mr Bathgate was in the next room. I decided against him as the victim—too obvious—then I heard the gong, and the lights went out. I was just going to call out that it couldn't be the "murder" but an accident of some sort, when I realized that I should be giving my own show away before I had brought it off. So I pretended to think it was the "murder" and began drying myself and dressing. I thought I should find an easy "victim" in the darkness.

I did too—!'

A violent exclamation from Handesley interrupted him.

'What is it, Sir Hubert?' asked Alleyn gently.

'It was you, then, Arthur, who ran into me on the landing and said, "You're the corpse"?'

'And it was you who answered "Shut up, you ass",' returned Wilde. 'Yes, you thought I was fooling. When I realized that, I got away quickly.'

'Just a moment,' interrupted the detective. 'Let me get this quite clear. Really it's frightfully muddling. When the alarm was given, Mr Wilde, you were in your bath. Knowing yourself to be the intended "murderer" in the game, you imagined the darkness and the gong sounding were accidental?'

'I thought the gong was sounded for dinner and that the lights had possibly fused.'

'Yes, I see. So you lay low and determined to perform your part in the game under cover of the dark?'

'Yes,' said Wilde. His voice was patiently courteous.

'For a detective,' thought Nigel, 'the inspector seems to be making rather heavy way of this.'

Alleyn continued. 'So you came out on to the landing, ran into Sir Hubert and instantly uttered the set phrase? You, Sir Hubert, thought he was fooling?'

'Yes, certainly. The signal had been given. As a matter of fact I thought—I rather thought it was Rankin. I don't know why.'

'Mr Wilde,' said Alleyn, 'in the words of the popular coloured engraving, when did you last see Mr Rankin?'

'I was talking to him alone in the hall before we went up to dress. We were the last to go up. Charles remarked that if either of us was "he" in the game, it would be no good trying to victimize the other, as everyone knew we were left alone together.'

'Yes, exactly. Then Mr Rankin was still in the hall

when you went up to dress?'

'Yes.'

'Did anyone see you together?'

Wilde thought for a moment. 'Yes,' he said, 'I remember Mary, the little between-maid, came in and went out to the entrance hall to lock the front door. She was still tidying or something as I went upstairs. I remember I asked her if she knew the right time—if the hall clock was right. She said, "Yes, ten minutes to eight"; and I said "Good lord, we'll be late", or something like that, and ran upstairs, leaving her there.'

'Presumably, then, Mr Rankin was alone in the hall from a little after seven-fifty till five minutes to eight, when he was killed. About four minutes. Thank you, Mr Wilde.'

Alleyn made a brief entry in his note-book and then looked round the table.

'Are there any questions that someone else would like to put?' he asked. 'I can assure you that I will honestly welcome them.'

There was a short silence, broken unexpectedly by Mrs Wilde. She leant across the table, looking with an odd air of formality at her husband.

'I would like to ask,' she said rapidly, 'what you and Charles talked about during the time you were alone together.'

For the first time Arthur Wilde hesitated.

'I don't think,' he said quietly, 'that we said anything that could have any bearing on the point at issue.'

'Nevertheless,' said Tokareff suddenly, 'the question is asked.'

'Well—' there was the faintest echo of whimsicality in his answer. 'Well, we talked about you, Doctor Tokareff.'

'Indeed? What about me?'

'Rankin seemed to resent your comments on his ownership of the dagger. He—he felt that it implied some sort of criticism of himself. He was rather on the defensive about it.'

Doctor Young unexpectedly uttered. his throaty comment—'Kaahoom'—and Alleyn smiled.

'What did you say to all this?' he asked.

Arthur Wilde rumpled up his hair. 'I told him not to be an ass,' he said. 'Charles was always rather touchy—it was characteristic. I tried to explain how a knife associated, as Doctor Tokareff believed, with the innermost ritual of a bratsvo, would naturally have more significance to a Russian than to an Englishman. He soon got over his huff and said he quite saw my point. Then we chaffed each other about the Murder Game and I left him.'

'Any more questions?' asked Alleyn.

There were none apparently.

'I realize,' said Wilde, 'that I was probably the last person—except Mary and the man who killed him—to see Charles alive. I hope very much that if anyone does think of any questions they would like to put, they will not hesitate in asking them.'

'I should like to say,' said Nigel, 'that I can corroborate most of what you have said. I left you with Charles and heard you come up a few minutes later. You remember we shouted out to each other while your bath was running and afterwards when the lights went out. I can state positively that you were in the bathroom before, during, and after the time when the crime was committed.'

'Yes,' agreed Marjorie Wilde, 'and you called through to me, too, Arthur.'

'Your rooms were all close together?' asked Alleyn.

Nigel sketched out a rough plan of the four rooms and slid it across the table to him.

'I see,' said the inspector, and looked carefully at it. 'I am sure you all appreciate,' he said a moment later, 'the importance of establishing Mr Wilde's account of his movements. They have already been corroborated by

Mrs Wilde and Mr Bathgate. Can anyone else bring forward any point that bears on the relative positions of these three after Mr Wilde came upstairs?'

'Yes,' said Mrs Wilde eagerly, 'I can. When I was in my room dressing, Florence, Angela's maid, came in to ask if she could help me. She stayed a few moments—not long—but she must have heard Arthur calling out and everything—the door into the bathroom wasn't shut properly.'

'She will be able to verify this herself, of course,' said the inspector. 'We have now a fairly complete picture of the movements of three of the house-party from shortly after seven-thirty until the time of the murder. Mrs Wilde went upstairs first, Mr Bathgate second, and Mr Wilde last. They were all calling out to each other while they were dressing, and their voices were probably heard by a housemaid. Mr Bathgate, I understand that you were the first downstairs after the alarm was given and that you turned up the lights?'

Nigel's thoughts had been wandering along a strange byway opened up by Mrs Wilde's eager corroboration of her husband's story. He pulled himself together and looked at the inspector. It struck him that the official manner came easily enough to Alleyn when he chose to assume it.

'Yes,' he said. 'Yes—I turned on the lights.'

'You found your way downstairs after the two minutes had elapsed?'

'Yes, the others were behind me on the stairs.'

'You got to the main switch and turned it on immediately?'

'Not immediately. The others were calling out from the stairs. I hesitated for a second.'

'Why?' asked Rosamund Grant.

'I really can't say. It was all rather strange and I felt— I don't know—somehow reluctant. Then Sir Hubert called out and I pulled down the switch.'

'You were talking to Mr Wilde right up to the time you left your room?'

'Yes, I think so.'

'Yes,' said Arthur Wilde, with a friendly glance towards him, 'you were.'

'Did you speak to anyone when you were on the landing?'

'I don't remember. Everyone was talking in the dark there. I struck a match.'

'Yes,' said Angela quickly, 'he struck a match. I was farther along the passage and saw his face suddenly lit up from beneath. He must have been just outside his room then.'

'Mr Bathgate,' said the detective, 'your match was still alight, wasn't it, as you went downstairs?'

'Yes. It went out about halfway down.'

'Did anyone pass you on the stairs?'

'No, nobody passed me.'

'Are you certain of that?'

'Quite positive,' said Nigel.

'Any more questions?' asked Alleyn.

Nobody spoke.

Inspector Alleyn turned to Tokareff.

'Doctor Tokareff,' he said, 'I shall take you next, if you please.'

'Thank you,' said the Russian pugnaciously.

'You went upstairs with the first detachment—Miss North, Miss Grant, Mrs Wilde, and Sir Hubert Handesley?'

Tokareff was glaring combatively through his spectacles at the detective.

'Certainly I did,' he said.

'Did you go straight to your room?'

'Yes, immediately. This I can prove, for I am in good mood while I am in my room last night, so I sing the *Death*

of Boris fortissimo. I am in distant wing of house, but still
my voice is robust. Many should have heard.'

'I heard,' said Handesley, and he actually smiled.

'Were you singing the *Death of Boris* all the time—until
the gong sounded and the lights went out?'

'Yes, certainly.'

'A gala performance! You visited a bathroom?'

'*Niet!* No! I do not bath at this hour. It is not advisable.
Better at night before bed, to open the pores. Then a
gentle sweat—'

'Yes, quite. You dressed then?'

'I dress. While I dress I sing. When I come to great cry
of agony, I interpret in the manner of Fedor Chaliapin—'
He suddenly gave tongue to a galvanizing bellow. Mrs
Wilde suppressed a little shriek. 'At this moment,' ended
Doctor Tokareff, 'gong goes and lights go out. It is the
game. I cease to sing and count sixty twice in Russian.
Then I come out.'

'Thank you very much. I understand that you were the
first to realize what happened to Mr Rankin?'

'Yes, I was first. I have seen the knoife from the stairs.'

'What happened then?'

'Miss Angela was saying in joking, "No one's to touch
the body". I was agreeing, not jokingly, because I have
seen the man is dead.'

'But I understand you did not examine the body—'

'Excuse me, please,' began the Russian with a great
deal of emphasis.

Alleyn glanced quickly round the table. A swift wave of
consternation and panic seemed to have galvanized the
faces of all the guests. Mrs Wilde was white to the lips and
Rosamund Grant was staring fixedly at her. Wilde leant
swiftly towards his wife. She spoke suddenly, her voice
breathlessly unlike the fashionable squeak that they were
all accustomed to.

'Wait a minute, I had better explain.'

'Never mind now, old girl,' said Wilde. Even then the conjugal endearment struck Nigel as being singularly inept.

'It's all right,' said Marjorie Wilde. 'I know what Doctor Tokareff is going to say. I lost my head. I pushed them all aside and knelt down by him. I pulled him over and looked at his face and I tried to call him back; when I saw he wasn't there any more, I tried to call him back, tried to force him to come back. I dragged his shoulders away from the blood, and I felt the knife gritting on the floor underneath him, gritting about inside him. He was very heavy, I only moved him a little way. They all said I wasn't to touch him—I wish I hadn't, but I did. I touched him.' She stopped as abruptly and breathlessly as she had begun.

'It was much better for you to tell me this at once, Mrs Wilde,' said Alleyn, very matter of fact. 'One quite appreciates the emotional stress and shock of this terrible discovery. I should like,' he continued generally, 'to fix the actual grouping of this scene in my mind. Mrs Wilde was kneeling beside the body. She had moved it over on to its back. Doctor Tokareff, you were standing beside her?'

'Certainly. I stood there saying, "Do not touch". Still she continued to shake at him. I have seen immediately that she is hysterical and I tried to raise her upwards, but she resisted me. In hysteria sometimes zere is sush a strength. Then Miss Grant said quite quietly, "It's no use to call Charles now, he is gone for good", and at once Mrs Wilde stopped. Then I have raised her away and Sir Hubert Handesley said, "For God's sake please make sure he is dead". I have known immediately that he is dead, but nevertheless I examine, and Miss North say, "Telephone Doctor Young", so she does.'

'Is everyone agreed that this is substantially correct?' asked Alleyn—formally.

There was a general murmur of assent.

'Since I prove that from seven-thirty to seven fifty-five I sing very loud in my room,' announced the Russian, 'is not this an Ali Baba? I should like now to go to London, where I have appointment for a meeting.'

'I am afraid that is impossible,' said Alleyn smoothly.

'But—' began the Russian.

'I will explain afterwards, Doctor Tokareff. At the moment we will see out the consummation of the Murder Game. Sir Hubert, what were your movements from the time you went upstairs until the alarm?'

Handesley looked at his own interlocked fingers lying before him on the table. He did not raise his eyes. His voice was even and unbroken.

'I went to my dressing-room at the far end of the corridor. I undressed and spoke to Vassily, who was putting out my things. Then he went out and I had my bath. I had finished bathing and had dressed—all except my dinner jacket—when there was a knock at my door. Angela came in. She wanted to know if I had any aspirin. Miss Grant had a headache and would like to take some. I found the aspirin and gave it to Angela. She went out and almost immediately afterwards the alarm sounded. I joined the party on the landing, and it was then that Arthur—Mr Wilde—tapped me on the shoulder and said, "You are the corpse." I think that is all.'

'Any questions?'

The vague negative murmur floated round the table.

'Miss Grant,' said the inspector, 'you also went upstairs with the first party. Where was your room?'

'At the far end of the cross-corridor at the back of the house, next to Angela's—to Miss North's. We went along together. Angela came into my room after we had bathed. It was then I asked her for aspirin.'

'Where is the bathroom you used?'

'Opposite my bedroom. We both used it—I first.'

'And you merely crossed the passage to this bathroom

and back to your own room?'

'Yes.'

'Did you go anywhere else while you were upstairs?'

'No. I came down after the alarm.'

'You, Miss North? What were your movements?'

'I came up with Rosamund. While she bathed I read in my own room. On my return from the bathroom I went in to her, and after that to my uncle's room for the aspirin. I had just got back to Rosamund's door when the lights went out.'

'Where is Mr Rankin's room?'

'Next to mine and immediately opposite the entrance of the top passage into the corridor. May I complete the sketch there?' Alleyn pushed the sheet of paper along to her, and she traced in the remaining rooms.

'Thank you very much,' said Alleyn. 'That completes the position of the characters. It also brings to a close the opening phase of the reconstruction of the game. Before we go I should like to speak to Florence your maid, Miss North. I am sure you will all see that it is most important to establish the positions of Mr and Mrs Wilde and Mr Bathgate.'

Angela got up and crossed to a bell-push by the mantelpiece. The others moved back their chairs, and Wilde began a low-voiced conversation with Händesley.

The bell was answered, not by Vassily, but by a small, agitated maid. She looked as if she belonged to the back stairs and had got into the drawing-room by mistake.

'Will you ask Florence to come in for a moment, Mary?' said Angela.

'Yes, miss.'

'Oh, just a second, Mary,' said Alleyn, with a glance at Angela. 'Were you in the hall last night when Mr Wilde went upstairs and Mr Rankin was left alone?'

'Oh—yes, yes, sir, I was. Mr Roberts don't usually send me to the front of the 'ouse, sir, but last night—'

'Did Mr Wilde speak to you?'

'He arst me the time, and I says, "Ten to", and he says, "Hell, I'm late", and skedaddles upstairs.'

'What was Mr Rankin doing?'

'Smoking a cigarette, sir, quite happy like. I says, "Shall I take away the cocktail tray?" and he says, "Don't do that," he says, "I'll have a quick one", he says, "and spoil the schoolboy complexion". So I goes away, sir, and then only a few seconds later, sir, the lights went out and—oh, isn't it awful?'

'Terrible. Thank you, Mary.'

After a hesitating glance at Handesley, the maid went out.

'Doesn't the butler usually answer that bell?' asked Alleyn after a pause.

'Yes,' said Angela vaguely—'yes, of course. Mary's the between-maid. She never answers the bell. I don't know why he didn't come—everyone is so upset, I suppose Vassily—'

She was interrupted by the entrance of Florence, a darkish wooden-faced individual of about thirty-five.

'Florence,' said Angela, 'Mr Alleyn wants to ask you something about last night.'

'Yes, miss.'

'Will you tell me, please,' began Alleyn, 'which of the rooms you went into last night when the guests were upstairs dressing?'

'Very good, sir. I went first to Miss Angela's room.'

'How long were you there?'

'Only a few minutes. Miss Angela wished to ask Mrs Wilde if I could assist her.'

'So you went to Mrs Wilde's room?'

'Yes, sir.'

'What happened there?'

'Madam asked me to fasten her dress. I fastened it,' said Florence sparsely.

'Did Mrs Wilde speak to you?'

'Madam was speaking to Mr Wilde, who was in the bathroom next door to the dressing-room.'

'Did Mr Wilde answer?'

'Yes, sir. He was speaking to Mrs Wilde and also to Mr Bathgate, who was in his own room beyond.'

'When you left Mrs Wilde, where did you go?'

'To Miss Grant's room.'

'How long were you there?'

'I waited a moment, sir. Miss Grant was not there. She came in a few minutes later and said she did not require me. I left. Miss Angela was coming along the passage. Then the lights went out.'

'Did Miss Grant come from the bathroom?'

Florence hesitated. 'I think not, sir. Miss Grant bathed earlier—before Miss Angela.'

'Thank you very much. I think that's all I wanted to ask you.'

'Thank you, sir.'

The door shut behind Florence. No one had looked at Rosamund Grant. No one had spoken.

Alleyn turned a page of his note-book.

'By the way, Miss Grant,' he said, 'did you not say that apart from your visit to the bathroom you did not leave your room until the gong sounded?'

'Wait a moment!' ejaculated Doctor Young.

'Rosamund—it's all right,' cried Angela, running across to her friend. But Rosamund Grant had slid from her chair to the floor in a dead faint.

In the sort of horribly false confusion that followed, Nigel was aware only of one thing, and that was the pounding at the bell-push in answer to some confused order of Sir Hubert's.

'Brandy—that's what she wants,' Handesley was shouting.

'Better some sal volatile,' said Doctor Young. 'Just

open those windows, one of ye.'

'I'll fetch some,' Angela said and hurried away.

The flustered Mary had reappeared.

'Tell Vassily to bring some brandy,' said Handesley.

'Please, sir, I can't.'

'Why not?'

'Oh, sir, he's gone — he's disappeared, sir, and none of us liked to tell you!'

'Hell's teeth!' ejaculated Alleyn.

CHAPTER 6

Alleyn Does his Stuff

Detective-Inspector Alleyn had been most particular about the state of the house. Nothing must be touched, he said, until he had finished what he called his nosey-parkering. Nothing had been touched. Little Doctor Young, in his capacity as police surgeon for the district, had stressed the point from the moment of his arrival, and Bunce, PC, in his brief and enjoyable supremacy, had scared the life out of the servants, keeping them all confined to their own quarters. He had, however, set no watch at the gate, and Vassily apparently escaped by the simple method of walking out at the back door.

Alleyn recovered from his momentary rage at the disappearance of the butler, rang up the station and found that the old Rusian had, with peculiar ingenuousness, caught the ten-fifteen for London. The inspector telephoned the Yard and gave orders that he should be traced and detained immediately.

By this time a detachment of plain-clothes men had appeared at Frantock. Alleyn had the tall and quite insurmountable fence inspected, mounted a guard of helmets,

felt hats and waterproofs at the gates, and invited
Detective-Sergeant Bailey, the fingerprint expert who had
come down with him, to attend him in the house. Mr
Bunce was also on tap in the hall. Handesley had been
requested to detain his guests in the library or to let them
loose in the garden.

'Now,' said Detective-Inspector Alleyn, 'I'll see Ethel,
the only housemaid remaining. Ask her to come in,
Bunce.'

Mary had been scared and Florence calm. Ethel, a
pretty girl of about twenty-seven, was intelligent and
interested.

'Where were you,' Alleyn asked her, 'at ten to eight
last night?'

'I was in my room upstairs, sir, at the end of the back
corridor. I had just changed my apron and noticed the
time, and I thought I would go downstairs and help Mary
tidy the hall. So I came along the back corridor into the
passage past the best bedrooms.'

'You mean past Mr Bathgate's room?'

'Yes, sir, that's right. I got as far as the head of the
stairs and looked over, and I saw Mr Rankin was still in
the hall. Mary was there too, sir, locking the front door,
and she looked up at me and jerked her head like, so I said
to myself that I'd wait till the hall was clear before I came
down. I turned back, and as I passed Mr Bathgate's door,
I remembered I hadn't brought his shaving water, and
that there was only two cigarettes left in his box. So I
tapped on the door.'

'Yes?'

'The door wasn't shut, and when I tapped it, it swung
in a bit like, and at the same time Mr Bathgate calls out.
"Come in". So I went in, and just as I was asking about
the shaving water the lights went out and I felt all
confused, sir, so I went out too, and kind of groped my
way back to my own room, sir.'

'What was Mr Bathgate doing?'

'Smoking a cigarette, sir, with a book in his hand. I think he had just called out something to Mr Wilde, who was bathing next door.'

'Thank you, Ethel.'

'Thank *you*, sir,' said Ethel plaintively. She withdrew with some reluctance.

Alleyn, with a mental shrug at Nigel's amazing imbecility in having overlooked his own cast-iron alibi, got on with the work. Roberts, the pantry-man, proved unprofitable. He had been in his pantry solidly for twenty minutes when the gong sounded. The cook and odd-boy were also completely without interest. Alleyn turned his attention to the hall itself.

He produced a tape measure and carefully took measurements between the cocktail table and the foot of the stairs. The tray with its sordid array of used glasses had been left untouched.

'All very nice and proper,' grumbled Alleyn to Detective-Sergeant Bailey; 'nothing disturbed except the minor detail of the body.'

'Lovely funeral if we'd only had a corpse, sort of,' responded Bailey.

'Well, young Bathgate says the body was lying at right angles to the gong. The last that Mary saw of Mr Rankin he was standing at the cocktail tray. Presumably at the end of it when he was struck. Come here, Bunce. How tall are you?'

'Five-foot-eleven in me socks, sir.'

'Good enough. The body is just on six foot. Stand here, will you?'

Bunce stood to attention, and Alleyn walked round him, looking at him carefully.

'What do you make of this, Bailey?' he said. 'This job was done inside five minutes at the most. The knife was in that leather slot by the stairs, unless it had been previously removed, which I think unlikely. Therefore, the murderer started off from here, took the thing in his right hand — so — and struck from the back.'

He went through the pantomime of stabbing the constable. 'Now see what I mean. I'm six-foot-two, but I can't get the right angle. Bend over, will you, Bunce? Ah, that's more like it; but the banister gets in the way. He may have been leaning over the tray. It's too far if I stand on the bottom step. Wait a bit. See if you can get anything from the bottom knob of the banister, will you, Bailey?'

'It'll be a fair mess of prints,' said the expert glumly. He opened a small grip and busied himself with the contents.

Alleyn nosed round the hall. He inspected the main switch, the glasses, the cocktail shaker, the gong, all the tables and woodwork. He paused by the grate. The dead clinkers of last night's fire were still there.

'I ses, "Don't you touch none of them grates",' said Bunce suddenly; 'there's only gas upstairs.'

'Quite right,' rejoined the inspector; 'we will deal with the fireplaces ourselves.' He bent over the fireplace and, taking a pair of tongs, removed the clinkers one by one, laying them on a piece of newspaper. As he did this he kept up a running commentary to Detective-Sergeant Bailey.

'You'll find Miss North's prints on that sketch plan of the house that I put on the tray there. Also Bathgate's. We must have everyone's, of course. The tooth-mugs upstairs will be profitable in that direction. I hate asking for prints, it makes me feel so self-conscious. There's nothing on the knife, needless to say — nor yet the switch. A nitwit wouldn't leave a print behind him nowadays if he could help it.'

'That's right, sir,' agreed Bailey. 'There's a proper muck up on the banister, but I rather think we'll get something a bit better from the knob.'

'The knob, eh?' said Alleyn, who had now drawn out
the ash-tray from under the grate.

'Curious position, too. There's a clear left-hand
impression pointing downwards. Quite an awkward place
to get your left hand, with the banister curving out at the
bottom the way it does. It's right on the inside edge. Very
clear, too. Saw it with me naked eye at once.'

'Your naked eye is uncanny, Bailey. Try the head of
the stairs. Hullo, what's this?'

He had been sifting the ashes in the tray, and now
paused, squatting on his heels and peering at a small
grimy object in the palm of his hand.

'Made a find, sir?' said the fingerprint expert, who was
now at work on the stair-head.

'Somebody's been chucking away their belongings,'
grunted the inspector. He produced a small magnifying
glass and squinted through it.

'A Dent's press button,' he murmured, 'with just a
fragment of—yes, of leather—charred, but unmistakable.
Ah, well.' He put his trophy in an envelope and wrote on
the flap.

The next twenty minutes he spent crawling about the
floor, standing on chairs to examine the stair-well and
outside of the treads, gingerly inspecting the cigarette
boxes, and directing Bailey to test the coal scuttle and fire
irons for prints.

'And now,' he said, 'for the bedrooms. The mortuary
van will be here any time now, Bunce. I'll leave you to
attend to that. Come on,' he said, and led the way
upstairs. On the landing he paused and looked about him.

'On our left,' he informed Bailey, 'the bedroom of Mrs
Wilde, the dressing-room of her husband, the bathroom,
and Mr Bathgate's room. All communicating. Very
matey and rather unusual. Well, begin at the beginning, I
suppose.'

Mrs Wilde's room was disordered and bore a faint

family likeness to a modern comedy bedroom. She had taken away its character, and Florence had not been allowed to put it back. The bed had not been made, and the early morning tea-tray was still on the table.

'There's your mark for prints, Bailey,' said the inspector, and once again the expert produced his bag.

'The alibi here is pretty good, I understand,' remarked Bailey, sifting a fine powder over the surface of a cup.

'Pretty good?' answered Alleyn. 'It's pretty damn' good for all of 'em except Miss Grant. She did tell a nice meaty lie about her movements, and followed up with a faint on top of it.'

He opened a suitcase and began going through the contents.

'What about this Russian affair, sir? The doctor or whatever he is?'

'Yes, he seems to be a likely horse. Do you fancy him, Bailey?'

'Well, from what you've told me about the knife and all that, it looks sort of possible. Personally I favour the butler.'

'If Tokareff's our man, he is pretty nimble on his pins. His room is some way along the passage and he sang, so they tell me, continuously. As for the butler—he was in the servants' quarters the whole time and was seen there.'

'Is that dead certain, sir? After all, he has done a bunk.'

'True. He is rather tempting; but when you've got your prints from the banister, I'll know better if I'm on the right track. Do your stuff in the bathroom now, will you, Bailey? Bathgate and Wilde will be found to predominate. Then come back and go through this tallboy for me while I get on to the other rooms. Do you mind working out of your department for a bit?'

'Pleasure, sir. What am I looking for?'

'A single glove. Probably yellow dogskin. Right hand. I

don't expect to find it here. Make a list of all the clothes, please.'

'Right, sir,' said Bailey from the bathroom.

Alleyn followed him and looked round the dressing-room and bathroom very carefully. Then he went to Nigel's room.

It was much as it had been the night before. The bed had not been slept in. Alleyn had learnt from Bunce that Nigel had been up all night, trying to get calls through to the family solicitor, to his own office, and, on behalf of the police, to Scotland Yard. He had been invaluable to Handesley and to Angela North, had succeeded in getting Tokareff to stop talking and go to bed, and had silenced Mrs Wilde's hysterics when her husband had thrown up his hands in despair and left her to it. The inspector considered Ethel's statement that she had actually seen Nigel in his room as the lights went out good enough proof of his integrity. However, he examined the room carefully.

Conrad's *Suspense* lay on the bedside table. The butts of two Sullivan Powell cigarettes were in the ash-tray. An inquiry showed that these were the last in the cigarette box at seven-thirty the evening before, and Ethel, recalled, repeated that she had noticed the box empty and Mr Bathgate smoking the last on her dramatically terminated visit. Mr Bathgate's own cigarettes were of a less expensive variety. 'Exit Mr Bathgate,' murmured the detective to himself. 'He couldn't smoke two cigarettes, commit a murder, and talk to a housemaid while he was doing it, in ten or twelve minutes.' He had come to this conclusion when the door opened and in walked Nigel himself.

At the sight of the Yard man in his room Nigel immediately felt as guilty as he would have done if his hands had been metaphorically drenched in his cousin's blood.

'I'm sorry,' he stammered, 'I didn't realize you were here — I'll push off.'

'Don't go,' said Alleyn amiably. 'I'm not going to put the handcuffs on you. I want to ask you a question. Did you by any chance hear anything outside in the passage while you were dressing last night?'

'What sort of thing?' asked Nigel, overwhelmed with relief.

'Well, what does one hear in passages? Any sound of a footfall, for instance?'

'No, nothing. You see, I was talking to Wilde all the time and his bath was running, too — I wouldn't have been able to hear anything.'

'I understand Mrs Wilde was in her room all this time. Do you remember hearing her voice?'

Nigel considered this carefully.

'Yes,' he said at last, 'yes, I am positive I heard Mr Wilde call out to her and I heard her answer him.'

'At what precise moment? Before or after the lights went out?'

Nigel sat on the bed with his head in his hands.

'I can't be certain,' he said at last. 'I'll swear on oath I heard her voice, and I *think* it was before *and* after the lights went out. Is it important?'

'Everything is important, but taken in conjunction with the icy Florence's statement, your own is useful as a corroboration. Now, look here, show me Tokareff's room, will you?'

'I think I know where it is,' said Nigel. He led the way down the passage into the back corridor and turned to the left. 'Judging from my recollection of his vocal efforts, I should say this was it.'

Alleyn opened the door. The room was singularly tidy. The bed had been slept in, but was little disturbed. Dr Tokareff would have appeared to have passed a particularly tranquil night. On the bedside table lay a Webster's

Dictionary, and a well-thumbed copy of *The Kreutzer Sonata* in English.

'Thank you so much, Mr Bathgate,' said Alleyn; 'I can carry on here.'

Nigel withdrew, thankful to leave the atmosphere of official investigation and yet, paradoxically, conscious of a sense of thwarted curiosity.

Inspector Alleyn opened the wardrobe and drawers and noted down the contents, then turned his attention to the suitcase that had been neatly bestowed under one of the cupboards. In this he found a small leather writing-case with a lock that responded at once to the attentions of a skeleton key. The case contained a number of documents typewritten in Russian, a few photographs, mostly of the doctor himself, and a small suede pouch in which he found a little seal set in a steel mount. Alleyn took it to the writing-table, inked it and pressed it down on a piece of paper. It gave a tolerably clear impression of a long-bladed dagger. The inspector whistled softly between his teeth and, referring to the documents, found a similar impression on many of the pages. He copied one or two sentences into his note-book, carefully cleaned the seal and replaced everything in the writing-case, snapping the lock home and restoring the suitcase to its former position. Then he wrote a note in his little book, 'Communicate with Sumiloff in re above,' and with a final glance round, returned to the passage.

Next he went into Angela's bedroom, and then into Rosamund Grant's. Finally he visited Sir Hubert Handesley's bedroom, dressing-room, and bathroom. All these he subjected to a similar meticulous search, making a list of the clothes, going through the pockets, sorting, examining, and restoring every movable and garment. He found little to interest him, and had paused to light a cigarette in Handesley's dressing-room, when a light rap on the door and a respectful murmur outside announced the presence of Detective-Sergeant Bailey.

Alleyn went out into the passage.

'Excuse me, sir,' said Bailey, 'but I think I've got hold of something.'

'Where?'

'In the lady's bedroom, sir. I've left it just as it is.'

'I'll come,' said Alleyn.

They returned to Marjorie Wilde's bedroom, passing Mary, all eyes, on the landing.

'Now then, Mary,' said Alleyn severely, 'what are you doing up here? I thought I asked you all to stay in your own department for an hour.'

'Yes, sir. I'm that sorry, sir, but the master's asked for 'is Norfick jacket wot's got 'is pipe in it, sir, and Mr Roberts 'e sent me up for it.'

'Tell Roberts I thought he understood my instructions. I will bring down the jacket myself for Sir Hubert.'

'Yes, sir,' murmured Mary plaintively, and scuttled downstairs again.

'Well, Bailey, what is it?' asked the inspector, shutting Mrs Wilde's door behind him.

'It's this drawer-contraption here,' said Bailey, with his slightly disparaging air of social independence.

The six drawers of a Georgian tallboy were laid out neatly on the floor.

'You've no eye for antiques, Bailey,' said Inspector Alleyn. 'That's a very nice piece indeed.' He walked over to the empty carcass and stroked the top surface appreciatively.

'It's a bit the worse for wear, however,' said Bailey. 'The casing at the bottom's hollow, and there's a hole in the inside lining. See, sir? Well, it seems to me someone's been scuffling about in that bottom drawer and pushed a small soft object over the end of it. It's fallen into the bottom. You can just touch it.'

Alleyn went down on his knees and thrust his fingers

into the gap in the bottom of the tallboy.

'Give me that buttonhook on the table,' he said quickly.

Bailey handed it to him. In a few minutes the inspector gave a grunt of satisfaction and fished up a soft, smallish object. He dropped it on the floor and stared at it with extraordinary concentration. It was a woman's yellow dogskin glove.

The inspector took an envelope out of his pocket and from it he produced a discoloured and blistered press button to which a few minute particles of leather were still adhering. He laid it beside the fastening on their find and pointed his long finger at the floor.

The two buttons were identical.

'Not such a bad beginning, Bailey,' said Inspector Alleyn.

CHAPTER 7

Rankin Leaves Frantock

After a brief cogitation Alleyn went over to the writing table and, laying the glove down, drew a chair up and sat in it, staring at his find as if it were some kind of puzzle for the correct solution of which a large prize was offered. He pursed his lips crookedly and twisted one long leg about the other. Finally, he took a rolled steel rule and a tape measure from his pocket and began to make elaborate measurements.

Bailey reassembled the tallboy, using methodical accuracy in the folding of each garment that it contained.

'Bring me one of the lady's gloves, will you?' grunted Alleyn suddenly.

Bailey selected a delicate trifle of fawn-coloured suède

and laid it on the writing table.

'Looks several sizes smaller to me,' he said, and turned back to his job.

'It is smaller; but, then, it's a different type,' rejoined the inspector. 'Your find is a sporting specimen. Mannish, tweeds-and-shooting-stick kind of thing. Indeed, a man with a moderate-sized hand could wear it.'

He smelt both the gloves, and looked for the makers' names.

'Same shop,' he said, and fell to making further measurements and noting them down in his book.

'That's that,' he said finally, and held out the suède glove to Bailey, who delicately replaced it.

'What about the other?' asked Bailey.

Alleyn deliberated.

'I think,' he said at last, 'I *think* I'll send it out to earn its keep. Have you finished in here?'

'Yes, sir.'

'Then carry on with the prints in the other rooms, will you? I'll join you · in Mr Rankin's room before lunchtime. Wait for me there.' He put the gloves in his pocket and went downstairs.

The hall was deserted except for Mr Bunce, who still kept watch and ward at the front door. Alleyn passed him and went into the entrance lobby. Mr Bunce revolved and stared trance-like through the glass partition. What was the god up to now?

One or two outdoor coats hung in the lobby, together with a collection of sticks and a pair of goloshes. Alleyn examined all these depressing objects closely, feeling in the pockets, writing in his inevitable book. The breath of Mr Bunce made a little mist upon the glass.

Finally, the inspector drew from his own pocket a yellow dogskin glove. He threw it on the bench, picked it up, cast it among the sticks, again retrieved it, and finally dropped it on the floor. Catching the eye of the constable,

and perhaps relishing his agonized curiosity, Alleyn laid
his finger on his lips and raised his left eyebrow. A spasm
of intense gratification passed across Mr Bunce's face,
succeeded by an expression of low cunning. 'This was
Ercles' vein,' Mr Bunce might have been thinking.
Alleyn took out his pipe and filled it. Then he opened the
glass door. Bunce fell back a pace.

'Where are the ladies and gentlemen?' asked Alleyn.

'Sir, in the garding,' said Bunce.

'What time's lunch?'

'One-fifteen.'

The inspector glanced at the clock. Five to one. A busy
morning. He returned to the porch, sat on the bench, and
for ten minutes smoked his pipe and did not so much as
glance at the constable. The porch became thick with
tobacco smoke. At five past one Alleyn opened the outer
door, knocked his pipe out on the edge of the stone step,
and remained staring out on to the drive.

Presently the sound of voices drifted in from the
garden. Alleyn darted back into the porch, and Bunce,
once more electrified, saw him take down two or three
coats and fling them on the floor. He was bending over
them when Handesley, Mr and Mrs Wilde, Angela and
Tokareff came up the front steps. They all stopped short
at the sight of the detective and a complete silence fell
among them.

'So sorry!' said Alleyn, straightening himself. 'I'm
afraid I'm very much in the way. Just been doing a little
routine work, Sir Hubert. I suppose it would be possible
for someone to hide behind these garments.'

There was more than a suggestion of enthusiasm in
Handesley's response. 'Yes—yes indeed, I should think
very possible,' he agreed quickly. 'Do you think that is
what may have happened? That someone came in from
outside before the door was locked and waited until—
until the opportunity arose?'

'That is a possibility that I myself have considered,' began the Russian. 'It is quite so clear as . . .'

'The door was still locked, wasn't it?' interrupted Alleyn, 'after the crime was committed?'

'Yes,' answered Handesley, 'yes, it was. Still, the murderer might have escaped in the dark by one of the other doors, surely?'

'It is worth considering,' agreed Alleyn. He hung up the coats, and in doing so dropped a yellow dogskin glove on the floor. He stooped and picked it up.

'An odd glove,' he said. 'I am afraid I have dropped it out of some pocket. So sorry. Any claimants?'

'It's yours, Marjorie,' said Angela suddenly.

'Why—so it is.' Mrs Wilde looked at it without touching it. 'I—it's mine. I thought I had lost it.'

'I don't see the other,' said Alleyn. 'This is the left hand. Don't say I've gone and lost the right.'

'It was the left I lost. I must have dropped it here.'

'Are you sure you did not leave them both down here, Mrs Wilde?' asked Alleyn. 'You see, if you did, and the right has gone, it might be worth tracing.'

'You mean,' said Handesley, 'that the right-hand glove might have been taken by—by the murderer when he hid here?'

'That sounds an interesting theory,' said Arthur Wilde. 'Darling, when did you miss this glove?'

'Oh, I don't know—how can I tell?' answered Marjorie Wilde breathlessly. 'Yesterday—yesterday we went for a walk—he and I. I had the right-hand glove then. He had given them to me—you remember, Arthur? —last Christmas. He teased me about losing it.' She turned blindly towards Wilde, who put his arm about her for all the world as though she were a child.

'Did you wear the single glove yesterday?' persisted Alleyn.

'Yes—yes, I wore it.'

'And when you came in, what did you do with it, Mrs Wilde?'

'I can't remember. It's not in my room.'

'Did you leave it here, do you think?' asked Angela gently. 'Marjorie, do *try* to think. I can see what Mr Alleyn means. It may be frightfully important.'

'I tell you I can't remember. I should think I did. Yes —I did. I'm sure I did. Arthur, shouldn't you think I did?'

'Darling heart!' said Wilde. 'I didn't see you; but I know you generally throw your gloves down as soon as you get in. I should take very long odds on it. The fact that the lost one was here,' he went on, turning to Alleyn, 'looks rather as if it was a favourite spot.'

'I think so, too,' said Alleyn. 'Thank you so much, Mrs Wilde. I'm very sorry to bother you.'

He opened the inner door, and Mrs Wilde and Angela went through followed by the men. Handesley paused.

What about luncheon, Mr Alleyn?' he said. 'I should be delighted if . . .'

'Thank you,' said Alleyn, 'but I think I will finish up here and in the bedrooms. The mortuary car will arrive at one-thirty. I should suggest, Sir Hubert, that you keep your guests as long as possible in the dining-room.'

'Yes, yes,' said Handesley, turning away quickly. 'I know what you mean. Yes, I will.'

Roberts, the pantry-man, came into the hall and announced lunch. Alleyn waited until they had all gone, pocketed the glove, and went upstairs to Rankin's room, where he found Bailey waiting for him.

'Any luck, sir?' asked the fingerprint expert.

'Not a great deal. The glove is Mrs Wilde's. She had lost it. Probably shoved it over the end of the drawer when she first came here. She wore the mate yesterday and the general idea is that she left it in the lobby downstairs. That may have been suggested by my supposedly finding the other one there. However, it seems quite likely. If she did, anyone may have picked it up. I've started a hare that our man may have come in from outside. You've seen how the ground lies there. Quite impossible, but it's useful to let them think it's our theory.'

'It would have been very easy for the butler to pick that glove up in the lobby or the hall and keep it by him,' said Bailey.

'Ah, your favourite. Yes, it would, and it would have been equally easy for any of the others to do so. Get out all the clothes, will you, Bailey? Blast. I had hopes of that glove.'

'The left-hand print on the stair knob is Mr Wilde's,' said Bailey.

'Is it?' answered Alleyn without enthusiasm. 'Aren't you a one?'

'It seems to me, sir,' said Bailey, as he opened the wardrobe doors, 'that whoever stabbed Mr Rankin took an enormous risk. Suppose he had turned and seen him.'

'If it was a member of the house-party, he had only to pretend he was the murderer in the game.'

'How was he to know Rankin wasn't the "murderer"?'

'It was an eight-to-one chance,' said Alleyn. 'Mr Wilde was the only one who would have been certain of that, and he was in his bath. Wait a moment, though—there was one other.'

'Yes, sir—Vassily.'

'One to you, Bailey. But Vassily wasn't playing.'

'Well, sir, I think he was.'

'I'm not at all sure I don't agree with you, you know. What have we here?'

Bailey had laid Rankin's suits out on the bed and was sprinkling the water-jug and glass with white powder. The two worked in silence for some time until Alleyn had come to the last of Rankin's garments—a dinner-jacket. This he carried over to the window and examined rather more closely.

'As a rule,' he observed, 'there is much less to be gleaned from the clothes of a man with a valet than from those of the poorer classes. "Highly recommended by successful homicide" would be a telling reference for any man-servant. Here, however, we have an exception. Presumably, Mr Rankin's valet sent him down here with a tidy dinner-jacket. By Saturday night he had managed to get a good deal of liquid powder down the face of it.'

'Keen on the ladies, I dare say,' said Detective-Sergeant Bailey placidly.

'Poor devil! There are certain aspects of our job that are not very delicious.'

Alleyn produced an envelope and a pocket knife. By dint of scraping the coat very delicately, he managed to collect a pinch of fine light powder.

'I may have to send the jacket in for analysis,' he said, 'but I think this will do. Go through all the papers now, Bailey, and the drawers. Then I think we have finished in here.'

He left his companion and returned to Mrs Wilde's, to Angela's, and to Rosamund Grant's rooms. On each of their dressing-tables he found collections of bottles and boxes. Mrs Wilde seemed to travel with half a beauty-parlour in tow. The inspector, who had collected a case from downstairs, opened it and produced a number of small bottles, into each of which he poured samples of liquid powder and of scent. These he carried back to Rankin's room and, picking up the dinner-jacket, nosed it reflectively.

'I rather fancy,' he said to Bailey, 'I rather fancy it's a mixture of "Milk of Gardenias" and "Chanel 5". Mrs Wilde and a hint of Miss Grant, in fact. But an analysis will correct me.'

'Someone,' said Bailey, 'has dusted the outer rim of the stairs and not the inner. There's a glove-mark on the knob. Did you notice, sir?'

'How you do dwell on those stairs!' said Alleyn.

And with that he finally left the bedrooms and went downstairs. In the hall he found Nigel.

'You have finished your lunch early, Mr Bathgate,' said Alleyn.

'I came out,' said Nigel. 'Sir Hubert told me what was happening, and I thought, if you didn't mind, that I would like to — to see Charles off.'

'Why, of course. I only thought that for the ladies it would be better to have it happen as unnoticeably as possible. Would you like to go into the study?'

'If I may, please.'

So Nigel stood and looked for the last time at Charles Rankin. He had never seen death before, but it seemed to him that it was not so very strange. Only he found it difficult to touch Charles, a gesture that obscurely he felt obliged to make. He put out his hand and met the cold heaviness of the forehead. Then he went back into the hall.

The mortuary car had arrived, and the men were already waiting. They brought Rankin out of the study, and in a very short time had driven him away. Inspector Alleyn stood by Nigel on the steps, watching until the car had disappeared down the drive. Nigel was conscious of him, and found that he liked his presence. When the sound of the car had died away, he turned to speak to the detective, but he had already gone. It was Angela who stood in the doorway.

'I know what's been happening,' she said. 'Come for a walk.'

'I'd like to,' said Nigel. 'Where shall we go?'

'I think the best thing we could do would be to go right round the home fields rather fast, and then finish up with a good go at badminton.'

'Right,' said Nigel, and they set off.

'We need a good deal of this sort of thing,' remarked Angela firmly, after they had walked in silence for some time, 'otherwise we'll all get morbid.'

'I should have thought with you that was an impossibility.'

'Well, you're wrong. There's a stream at the bottom of this field. If it's not too sloppy we can jump across. What were we saying? Oh, yes. Me and morbidness. I do assure you I could easily become as grim as a Russian novel. Oh, for heaven's sake, don't let's talk about Russians! Doctor Tokareff is positively deafening, I find.'

'He is rather fatiguing.'

'Nigel!' said Angela suddenly. 'Let's make a pact. Let's be honest with each other—about the murder, I mean. It'll help such a lot. Do you agree? Or am I a nuisance?'

'I agree. I'm so glad you've suggested it, Angela; and how could you possibly be a nuisance?'

'Well, then, that's all right. I don't think you killed Charles. Do you think I did?'

'No,' said Nigel.

'Who do you think did it?'

'Honestly, I *can't* think.'

'But,' insisted Angela, 'you must have leanings—you must.'

'I suppose, then, I lean towards Vassily, although he did seem such an honest-to-God old chap.'

'Yes, I know,' agreed Angela. 'I sort of *think* Vassily did it, but I don't *feel* he did.'

'Who do you feel did it, Angela? Don't answer if you'd rather not.'

'It's part of the pact.'

'I know,' said Nigel, 'but don't if you'd rather not.'

They had reached the tiny stream that ran across the bottom of the field. The ground on either side was muddy and dappled with small puddles.

'I want to,' said Angela, 'but it'll be rather like crossing the stream to do it.'

'Let me carry you across.'

'I don't mind getting muddy.'

'But I mind if you do. Let me carry you!'

Angela looked at him. 'What's all this?' thought Nigel confusedly. 'I've only just met her. What's happening?'

'Very well,' said Angela, and put one arm round his neck.

Liquid mud flowed into his brogues, and water struck like ice at his ankles. Neither of these discomforts did he resent, and when they reached firm ground he walked on delightedly until they had approached the trees.

'You may put me down,' said Angela, close to his ear.

'At once,' she added, rather loudly.

'Yes, certainly,' said Nigel, and obeyed.

'Now,' continued Angela, pink in the face, 'having crossed the stream, I'll tell who I feel—'

'Wait a moment,' said Nigel suddenly.

From behind them on the home side of the field a voice was hailing him.

'Mr Bath—gate!'

They turned and saw Mrs Wilde waving energetically.

'There's a telephone call come through for you from London,' shouted Mrs Wilde.

'Damn!' muttered Nigel. 'Thank you!' he shouted.

'You'll have to go back,' said Angela. 'I'll go round the long way to the barn.'

'But you haven't told me—'

'I don't think, after all, that I will,' said Angela.

CHAPTER 8

Following Information from a Baby

Nigel's long-distance call turned out to be from Mr Benningden the family solicitor. Mr Benningden was one of those small, desiccated gentlemen so like the accepted traditional figure of a lawyer that they lose their individuality in their perfect conformation to type. He was greatly perturbed by Charles Rankin's death. That Nigel, who knew him very well, could be sure of; but his dry voice and staccato phrases had lost nothing of their formal precision. He arranged to come down to Frantock the following afternoon. Nigel hung up the receiver, and went to the barn in search of Angela.

Halfway there he ran into Alleyn, who was talking to an under-gardener. Evidently the inspector had extended his examination of the servants to the outdoor staff. Nigel remembered how yesterday the guests had wandered off in twos and threes. He had seen Mrs Wilde and Rankin in the garden, and had wondered if Wilde and Rosamund were together. Would Alleyn try to trace the movements of each individual? Was there any significance in the grouping? What, wondered Nigel, not for the first time, what exactly *was* the inspector up to? The under-gardener held by the hand a very small, very dirty, very red-faced child of undecipherable sex, whom Alleyn was regarding with a comical air of frustration.

'Mr Bathgate,' ejaculated the inspector. 'One moment! Tell me, have you a way with children?'

'I really don't know,' said Nigel.

'Well, don't hurry away like that. This is Stimson, the third gardener, and this is his daughter—er—Sissy. Sissy

Stimson. Stimson tells me that she returned yesterday from the woods full of some story of a weeping woman. I rather want to investigate, but she is a difficult witness. Do see if you can have a success with her. I want to settle the identity of this tearful lady, and also of a person who appears to have trotted along beside her. Sissy is not exactly a gossipy child. Er, Sissy—here's Mr Bathgate come to talk to you.'

'Hullo, Sissy,' said Nigel reluctantly.

Sissy flung herself at her father's leg and buried her face in his unappetizing trousers.

'Cut that out,' said Stimson. 'She's a peculiar child, sir,' he continued, turning to Nigel. 'A very peculiar nature she's got. Now, if her Ma was present, I don't doubt but what she's have the whole matter out of Sissy; but unluckily, sir, the wife's away till Saturday, and I can't say I've got the same light touch with the child. Here, give over, will 'ee, Sis.'

He moved his leg uneasily, but the little girl refused to detach herself.

'Sissy,' said Nigel, feeling inadequate and ridiculous, 'would you like a nice silver penny?'

A baleful eye showed round a fold of the trousers. Nigel produced a shilling and held it up with an air of simulated ecstasy.

'Look what I've found,' he simpered.

A sort of falsetto growl rose from the truculent child.

'Gatcha!' it said.

'Go on,' said Alleyn. 'Splendid! Go on.'

'Would you like this silver penny?' inquired Nigel, squatting on his heels and holding the shilling very close to the child's face.

Sissy made a sudden grab, and Nigel snatched back his hand.

' 'Tain't a penny—it's a shillun,'' said Sissy derisively.

'So it is!' agreed Nigel. 'Well, look here, I'll give it to

you if you'll tell this nice gentleman—' he shot a vindictive glance at Alleyn—'what you saw in the woods yesterday.'

Dead silence.

'Oh!' squeaked the inspector suddenly, 'I've found a silver shilling, too. Fancy!'

Stimson showed signs of enthusiasm.

'Come on, carn't 'ee!' he urged his daughter. 'Speak up, Sis. Tell the gentleman all about that theer lady that was crying in the coppice; they'll give you a coupla bob. There now!'

Sissy had come out of cover and was swinging her barrel-like body from side to side.

'Was she a big lady?' asked Alleyn.

'Nah!' whined Sissy.

'Was she a little lady?' asked Nigel.

'Nah!'

'Well, now, approximately—' began the inspector, and checked himself. 'Was she alone?' he inquired.

'I seen a loidy,' said Sissy.

'Yes, yes. Excellent. So far, so good. Now, was this lady alone? All alone!' chanted Alleyn in a sort of faraway croon. 'All alone!'

Sissy stared at him.

'Was she—was she all by 'elf?' asked Nigel, trying baby talk.

'Nah! said Sissy.

'There was someone else with the lady?'

'Yea-us.'

'Another lady?' suggested Nigel.

'Nah. Loidies don't go wiv loidies in der coppus.'

Stimson laughed coarsely. 'Isn't she a masterpiece, sir?' he asked.

'Come now,' said Alleyn crisply. 'We are getting on. The lady was with a gentleman?'

Nigel had to repeat this question.

'Yea-us,' conceded Sissy.

'What sort of gentleman?' began Alleyn.

Sissy made another grab at Nigel's shilling and gave a sudden boisterous shout.

'Was he a big gentleman?' said Nigel, backing away from her.

'Gimme der shillun!' yelled Sissy. 'Yah! Gimme der shillun!'

'No!' said Nigel. 'Not if you aren't a good girl.'

The girl screamed piercingly and flung herself face downwards on the path, where she remained yelling and thrashing about with her legs.

'That's tore it,' said Stimson gloomily.

'What are you doing to that poor baby!' cried an indignant voice, and Angela came hurrying down the path. In a moment she was kneeling on the ground and had gathered Sissy up in her arms. The child clung round Angela's neck and buried her filthy little face in her blouse.

'Toike away the nasty gentlemen!' she sobbed, 'and gimme der shilluns!'

'My poor darling,' crooned Angela. 'Why have you been teasing her?' she demanded fiercely of Nigel and Alleyn.

'We haven't been doing anything of the sort,' said Nigel crossly. 'Have we, Stimson?'

'You didn't go for to, sir,' agreed Stimson. 'It's like this, miss,' he continued. 'Sissy saw a lady and gentleman in the coppice, and the lady was crying, and this gentleman wants to know the rights of it. And young Sis, she's turned rancid on us, miss.'

'I don't wonder,' said Angela. 'Give me that money you've been tormenting her with.'

Alleyn and Nigel handed over the shillings.

'There, my precious!' murmured Angela. 'We won't tell them anything about it. We'll have it for a secret. You whisper to me what the silly old people in the woods were like. You needn't wait, Stimson. I'll bring her along to the cottage.'

'Very good, miss,' said Stimson, and retired.

Sissy appeared to blow ferociously in Angela's ear.

'A lady with a lovey red cap,' whispered Angela. 'Poor lady! I expect a wopsie had bitten her, don't you? Was it a big gentleman?'

Alleyn had whipped out his note-book. Sissy was breathing hard into Angela's hair.

'It was a funny gentleman,' reported Angela. 'Why was he funny? Just funny. You saw another lady this afternoon, did you? What was she doing, darling? Just walking. There now! That was a lovely secret, and now we'll go home.'

'I've got a lovely secret, too,' said Detective-Inspector Alleyn astonishingly.

Sissy, who had detached herself from Angela, turned a watery eye on him. The inspector suddenly squatted down by her and distorted his face slightly so that one slim black eyebrow shot up his forehead. Sissy chuckled. The eyebrow came back to normal.

'More!' said Sissy.

'It won't do it again unless you whisper to it some more about the gentleman you saw in the coppice,' said Alleyn.

Sissy waddled across the path and placed a fat, earthy paw on the inspector's face. He flinched slightly and shook his head. Sissy whispered. The eyebrow moved up.

'There! That's how it works,' remarked Alleyn; 'and if we went into the coppice, there's no knowing if it wouldn't do it again.'

Sissy looked over her shoulder at Angela. 'Doin' to der coppus,' she said briefly.

Alleyn rose with the child in his arms.

'Leave to dismiss, Miss North?' he asked politely.

'Certainly, Inspector Alleyn,' said Angela stiffly.

The inspector peformed a guardsman's salute with his free hand, and strode off down the path with Sissy's arms entwined lovingly about his neck.

'Extraordinary!' said Nigel.

'Not a bit,' rejoined Angela. 'The child has got sense, that's all.'

'Shall we play badminton?' asked Nigel.

'By all means,' responded Miss North.

Alleyn's first action on returning to Frantock from his session with Miss Stimson was to wash himself very thoroughly in the downstairs cloakroom. He then looked up one of his notes made during what he called 'wardrobe inspection' that morning, read a certain entry in reference to a red cap, and inquired of Ethel if he could speak to Miss Grant. He learned that Doctor Young was attending her in her room.

'I will wait for Doctor Young,' said Alleyn, and sat down in the hall.

He had not been there long before Wilde came in from the garden. He hesitated, as indeed they all did, at the sight of the inspector, and then asked if he was waiting for anyone.

'I'm really waiting for Doctor Young,' said Alleyn, 'but I also wanted to see Sir Hubert. I wonder, Mr Wilde, if you know where he is?'

The archaeologist rubbed his hair up the wrong way — a characteristic gesture.

'He *was*—in there,' he said, pointing to the study door.

'In the study?'

'Yes.'

'Really? I must have missed him somehow,' remarked the inspector ambiguously. 'When did he go in?'

'Soon after they took—Charles—away,' said Wilde. 'He may still be there. Would you like me to ask if he can see you, Inspector?'

'Thank you so much,' said Alleyn gratefully.

Wilde opened the study door and looked inside. Evidently Handesley was still there, as Wilde went in and Alleyn heard their voices. He waited a couple of minutes, and then Wilde appeared again. Alleyn thought he looked faintly shocked.

'He is just coming,' he said, and with a nod to the inspector went upstairs.

Handesley came out of the study. He had a sheet of note-paper in his hand.

'Ah, there you are, Inspector,' he said. 'I have just been going through a few papers that I wanted.' He hesitated, and then went on with painful deliberation, 'It was impossible for me to enter the room while Mr Rankin's body lay there.'

'I can well understand that,' said Alleyn.

'This,' continued Handesley, holding out the paper, 'is the document I mentioned this morning. The will Mr Rankin signed yesterday, bequeathing the dagger to me. You mentioned that you would like to see it.'

'You have made things easy for me, Sir Hubert,' said Alleyn. 'It was in my mind to ask you for it.'

He took the paper and read it through impassively.

'I suppose,' said Handesley, who was staring out at the front door, 'I suppose that, although the thing was drawn up more or less in fun, it does actually constitute a legal document?'

'I am no lawyer,' answered Alleyn, 'but I should imagine that it was quite in order. May I keep it for the moment?'

'Yes, of course. I suppose later on I may have it again? I should like to keep it.' He paused, and then added quickly, 'You see, it is the last thing he wrote.'

'Certainly,' said Alleyn imperturbably.

Doctor Young appeared and came downstairs.

'May I see your patient, Doctor Young?' asked Alleyn.

The doctor performed the feat known in Victorian nursery books as "looking grave".

'She's not so grand,' he said doubtfully. 'Is it necessary?'

'Shouldn't ask you if it wasn't,' rejoined Alleyn quite amicably. 'I won't keep her long, and I've a beautiful bedside manner.'

'She's in a very highly strung condition. I'd rather she was left to herself for a bit — but, of course —'

'Of course Mr Alleyn must see her,' Handesley broke in. 'This is no time for attacks of the vapours, Doctor Young.'

'Well, Sir Hubert —'

'I feel really strongly about it,' said Handesley emphatically. 'Rosamund is a young woman of character; she is most unlikely to give in to her nerves. The sooner the inspector gets through his job, the better for all of us.'

'I wish everyone else felt the same way about it,' said Alleyn. 'I won't be ten minutes, Doctor Young.' And he went upstairs without waiting for the little doctor to answer him.

In response to his knock at her door, Rosamund Grant called out in her usual strong, rather deep voice. He went in and found her lying in bed. Her face was terribly white, and all the colour seemed to have been drained out of her lips. But she was cool enough when she saw who her visitor was, and invited him to sit down.

'Thank you,' said Alleyn. He drew up a small armchair, and seated himself between the bed and the window.

'I'm sorry you are laid up, Miss Grant,' he said in his matter-of-fact way, 'and sorrier still to disturb you. I have often wondered which is the more indecently preposterous job — a detective's or a journalist's.'

'You should compare notes with Nigel Bathgate,' rejoined Rosamund Grant. 'Not,' she added wearily, 'that he's been trying to get stories out of us. I suppose even the keenest journalist does not try to make copy out of his cousin's murder, especially when he happens to be his cousin's heir.'

'Mr Bathgate is the only member of this household from whom I have definitely withdrawn suspicion,' said Alleyn.

'Indeed,' she answered harshly. 'And do I head the list of suspects, Inspector Alleyn?'

Alleyn recrossed his legs and appeared to deliberate. Had a third person been there at Rosamund Grant's bedside, he might have thought to himself how strangely secret are the thoughts of human beings. Impossible to read what mental agonies tormented the mind of this pale harsh woman. Impossible to see behind the shadowy face of the detective into the pigeon-holes of his brain.

'I think,' he said at last, 'I think you were ill-advised to mislead me at the mock trial this morning. That sort of thing creates a very bad impression. Far better to tell me where you went after your bath last night. You did not go to your room. Florence saw you returning to it from somewhere along the corridor. Miss Grant—where had you been?'

'Has it not occurred to you that—that there might be a perfectly natural and obvious explanation that it would have embarrassed me to give at our mock trial?' said Rosamund.

'Oh, nonsense,' answered Alleyn crisply. 'You are not the type to recoil upon Victorian gentility with a charge of this sort under discussion. That I don't believe. Tell me where you went, Miss Grant. I cannot force you to answer, but I do earnestly advise you to do so.'

Silence.

'Then tell me,' said Alleyn, 'with whom you went walking in the woods, wearing your red cap, and weeping so bitterly.'

'I can't tell you,' said Rosamund fiercely. 'I can't—I can't.'

'As you please.' Alleyn appeared to be suddenly indifferent. 'Perhaps before I go you will let me have a few more details about yourself.' He produced his notebook. 'How long have you known Mr Rankin?'

'Six years.'

'Quite a long friendship—you could have scarcely been grown up when you first met.'

'I was at Newnham; Charles was nearly twenty years older than I.'

'At Newnham?' said Alleyn, politely interested. 'You must have been up with a cousin of mine—Christina Alleyn.'

Rosamund Grant waited for some seconds before she answered him.

'Yes,' she said at last, 'yes—I remember her, I think.'

'She is a fully-fledged chemist now,' he told her, 'and lives in an ultra-modern flat in Knightsbridge. Well, I shall be flayed alive by Doctor Young if I stay here any longer.' He got up and stood over the bed. 'Miss Grant,' he said, 'be advised by me. Think it over. I shall come here tomorrow. Make up your mind to tell me where you went to immediately before Mr Rankin was murdered.'

He walked to the door and opened it. 'Think it over,' he repeated, and went out.

Marjorie Wilde and her husband were standing in the passage.

'How is she?' asked Mrs Wilde quickly. 'I want to go in and see her.'

'Not a hope, I'm afraid. It's strictly against orders,' answered Alleyn cheerfully.

'There you are, Marjorie,' said Wilde. 'What did I tell you? Wait till you've seen Doctor Young. I am sure Rosamund does not want visitors.'

'You saw her!' said Mrs Wilde to Alleyn. 'I should have thought that would be worse than any ordinary visitor.'

'Marjorie darling!' ejaculated Wilde.

'Oh, everybody loves a policeman,' remarked Alleyn. 'She was thrilled to see me.'

'Marjorie!' called Angela's voice from the stairs.

Mrs Wilde looked from her husband to the inspector.

'Marjorie!' called Angela again.

'Coming!' answered Mrs Wilde suddenly. 'I'm coming!' And she turned away and walked quickly towards the stairs.

'Sorry about that,' said Wilde, looking troubled. 'She's not exactly herself, and she had made up her mind to see Miss Grant. It's a horrible experience for a woman, all this.'

'It is, indeed,' agreed Alleyn. 'Are you coming down, Mr Wilde?'

Wilde glanced at the closed door.

'Yes, certainly,' he said, and they went down together.

Alleyn had finished at Frantock for the time being, but he did not yet feel entitled to call it a day. His next move was to the police station at Little Frantock, where he put through a long-distance call to London. He waited a minute and then spoke into the receiver:

'Christina!' he said. 'Is it yourself! What a bit of luck! Look here, you can help me if you will. It's your cousin the policeman, and he's up agin it, my dear. Drag your mind away from shattered atoms and bicarbonate of soda, cast it back six years, and tell me everything—everything you can remember about one Rosamund Grant who was up at Newnham with you.'

A miniature voice crackled in the ear-piece.

'Yes,' said Alleyn, getting out his pencil and straightening the message block by the telephone, 'yes.'

The voice crackled on. Alleyn extended his call. He wrote busily, and gradually a curious expression—eager, doubtful, intensely concentrated—stole over his face. It was a look with which they were very familiar at the Yard.

CHAPTER 9

Garden Piece

'If you don't mind,' said Nigel to old Mr Benningden, 'I'll walk as far as the front gates with you.'

'Pleasure, my dear fellow,' replied the lawyer, with hurried cordiality. He snapped the catch of his grip, took off his pince-nez, eyed them severely, gave Nigel a quick glance, and took his coat and hat from the attendant Robert.

'Come along,' he said decisively, and made for the door.

'You were always an imaginative, sensitive sort of individual,' said Mr Benningden, as they walked down the drive. 'I remember your mother worrying her head off about it; but I put it to her that your boyish troubles were as short-lived as they were distressing. You will soon get over your ridiculous antipathy to accepting this bequest.'

'It's all so beastly,' said Nigel. 'I know they can't suspect me in any way, but—I dunno. It's not that so much as the idea of it. Benefiting by a filthy murder.'

'Sir Hubert Handesley and Mr Arthur Wilde are also legatees—they probably feel very much the same about it, but of course they have approached the matter in a much more sensible manner. Do you follow their example, my dear Nigel.'

'Very well. I'll be jolly glad of the money in a way, of course.'

'Of course, of course. Do not suppose that I am insensible of the delicacy of your position.'

'Oh, Benny!' said Nigel, half affectionate and half irritated, 'do stop talking like the old family lawyer.

Really, you are quite incredible!'

'Indeed?' said Mr Benningden amicably. 'It has become automatic, possibly.'

They walked on in silence until Nigel asked him abruptly if he knew anything in his cousin's life that could throw light on the murder.

'I don't want you to betray any secrets, of course,' he added quickly; 'you wouldn't pay much attention if I did. But had Charles an enemy or enemies?'

'I have been asking myself that question ever since this dreadful crime took place,' replied Mr Benningden, 'but I can think of nothing. Your cousin's relationships with women were, shall we say, of a slightly ephemeral nature, my dear Nigel; but so are those of many bachelors of his age. Even this aspect of his life, I hoped, was soon to be stabilized. He came to me two months ago and, after a good many circumlocutions, gave me to understand he was contemplating matrimony. I think I may safely go so far as to say he asked one or two questions about a marriage settlement, and so on.'

'The devil he did!' ejaculated Nigel. 'Who was the girl?'

'My dear boy, I *don't* think—'

'Was it Rosamund Grant?'

'Really, Nigel—well, in confidence, after all, why not? Yes, Miss Grant's name was—ah, it did arise in this connection.'

'Has he mentioned it more recently?'

'I ventured to bring it up a fortnight ago when he consulted me about renewing the lease of his house. He replied, as I thought, rather oddly.'

'What did he say?'

Mr Benningden swung his umbrella out in front of him as though he were pointing it at his own statement.

'He used, as far as I can recollect, these very words: 'It's no go, Benny; I've been caught poaching and I've

lost my licence.' I asked him what he meant by that, and
he laughed, very bitterly I thought, and said that
marriage with a woman who understood you was
emotional suicide, a phrase that had the advantage of
sounding well and meaning nothing.'

'Was that all?'

'I pressed him a little further,' said Mr Benningden
uncomfortably, 'and he said that he had made an enemy
of a woman who still loved him, and added something
about grand-opera passions and his own preference for
musical comedy. He seemed very sour and, I thought,
almost alarmed.

'The subject was dropped, and we did not refer to it
again until he was leaving. I remember as he shook hands
with me he said, "Goodbye, Benny. Control your
curiosity. I may promise to reform, but it'll be the death
of me if I do".'

Mr Benningden stopped short and stared at Nigel.

'He said this quite gaily and irresponsibly,' he added.
'It has only just occurred to me how strangely it may
sound now that he is dead. Ah, well, it's of no consequence,
I dare say.'

'Probably not,' agreed Nigel abstractedly. 'There are
the gates, Benny. Let me know if there is anything I can
do.'

'Yes, yes, of course. I am meeting Detective-Inspector
Alleyn at the police station. He is a very able man, Nigel.
I feel sure your cousin's death will not go unavenged.'

'I am afraid,' said Nigel, 'that in this respect I too have
little of the grand-opera instinct. My one hope is that
Charles was not murdered by any of his friends. That old
butler, the Russian—why don't the police do something
about him?'

'I feel sure they are doing quite a lot in that direction,'
rejoined Mr Benningden drily. 'Goodbye, my dear
fellow. I shall be down for the inquest, of course. In the

meantime, goodbye.'

Nigel walked slowly back towards the house. The prospect of spending the rest of the afternoon indoors was not an attractive one. The house-party lived on with a horrible posthumous individuality. The grotesque nature of their enforced familiarity was beginning to tell on the nerves of all the guests. Nigel was conscious of strange and hideous suspicions working like a ferment in their minds. Frantock had become envenomed. He longed to get away from it, and with this idea at the back of his head, turned off the drive and walked down a side path towards the wood. He had not gone far when a bend in the path revealed a green bench and sitting on it, curiously huddled, the figure of Rosamund Grant.

Nigel had seen very little of her since the tragedy. As soon as the official inspection of their rooms was over, Angela and Doctor Young had taken her upstairs, and there she had stayed, as far as Nigel knew, ever since. She raised her head now and caught sight of him. Feeling that he could not turn back, and conscious of the horrible restraint that came between himself and all of them, he walked up to her and made some conventional inquiry about her health.

'Better?' she said in her deep voice with its falling inflexion. 'Oh, yes, I'm better, thank you. I shall be joining your jolly party downstairs in time for the inquest on your cousin's murder.'

'Don't!' said Nigel.

She flung herself back impatiently.

'Have I dropped a brick?' she said. 'Do you cut the murder dead among yourselves? Angela and I talk about it, or rather Angela talks and I listen. She is a peculiar person, Angela.'

Nigel did not answer. She stared at him fixedly.

'Of what are you thinking?' she asked. 'Are you wondering if I killed him?'

'We all wonder that about each other, all day and half the night,' said Nigel brutally.

'I don't.'

'You are the more fortunate.'

'I only wonder what that man Alleyn is doing, what he is building up out of the mass of detail, what neat, ugly conclusion he is coming to. They say the Yard is never wrong in its inferences, though it sometimes fails to get its results. Do you believe this?'

'My only information is based on detective fiction,' said Nigel.

'So is mine.' Rosamund laughed silently, shrugging up her thin shoulders. 'And nowadays they make their Yard men so naturalistic that they are quite incredible. This man Alleyn, with his distinguished presence and his cultured voice and what-not, is in the Edwardian manner. He hectors me with such *haute noblesse* it is quite an honour to be tortured. Oh God, oh God, I wish Charles were not dead!'

Nigel was silent, and after a moment she began to speak again.

'A week ago,' she said, 'no, three days ago — I thought to myself, quite seriously, you know, that I should be glad if I knew I was going to die. Now — now I am terrified.'

'What do you mean?' Nigel broke out, and at once checked himself. 'No — don't tell me without being sure you won't wish that you hadn't.'

'I'll tell you this much,' she said; 'it is not the detective that I am afraid of.'

'Then why don't you go to him and make a clean breast of whatever it is?'

'What! Betray myself!'

'I don't understand you,' said Nigel heavily. 'Why can't you tell Alleyn what you did when you went upstairs? Nothing can be more dangerous than your silence.'

'Suppose I said I went in search of Charles?'

'That? For what reason?'

'Someone is coming,' she said quickly.

There was indeed the sound of a light footstep beyond the trees. Rosamund stood up as round the bend in the path came Marjorie Wilde.

She was wearing a black overcoat, but had no hat on. When she saw them she stopped dead.

'Oh—hullo,' she said. 'I didn't know you two were out here. Are you better, Rosamund?'

'Yes, thank you,' answered Rosamund, staring at her. A heavy silence fell among them. Mrs Wilde suddenly asked Nigel for a cigarette.

'We have been having a cosy chat about the murder,' said Rosamund. 'Who do you think did it?'

Mrs Wilde laid her hand to her cheek, and her lips parted, showing a line of clenched teeth. Her voice usually so shrill, came at last on an indrawn breath.

'I can't understand you—how can you talk of it like this—or at all?'

'You are acting the woman who has been deeply shocked,' said Rosamund. 'You are feeling it too, I expect, but not in the way you want to convey to us.'

'How like you!' exclaimed Mrs Wilde. 'How like you to talk and talk, silly clever stuff that makes you feel superior. I am sick of cleverness.'

'We are all sick of each other,' said Nigel desperately, 'but for the love of Mike don't let's say so too often. Saying things makes them so real.'

'I don't care how often I say who did this thing,' answered Mrs Wilde quickly. 'It is obvious. Vassily did it. He was furious with Charles for having that knife. He never liked Charles. He's run away. Why don't they get him, and let us all go?'

'I'm off,' said Rosamund suddenly. 'Doctor Young is coming at four-thirty to get on with his cure for the after-

effects of murder. ''The mixture as before''.' She walked
away quickly, as if she were escaping from something.

'Have you seen Arthur anywhere?' asked Mrs Wilde.

'I believe he's indoors,' replied Nigel.

'I *do* think men are extraordinary.' This was evidently
a stock phrase of Mrs Wilde's. 'Arthur doesn't seem to
realize how I feel about it all. He leaves me by myself for
hours at a time while he and Hubert read up the history of
Russian politics. It is really rather selfish of him, and
what good can it do?'

'It may have a good deal of bearing on the case,
surely,' said Nigel.

'I should have thought — oh, there he is,' she broke off.
Her husband had come out on to the terrace, and was
walking slowly up and down, smoking. She hurried away
towards him.

'Poor Arthur!' murmured Nigel to himself.

He walked on, down the path which described a wide
detour, fetching up at the entrance to the orchards at the
back of the house. The pleasant, acrid smell of burning
leaves hung on the air.

Beyond the orchard wall where the woods straggled out
in a fringe of thickets, a narrow spiral of blue smoke
wavered and spread into thin wisps. He wandered round
the outside of the orchard towards it. As he turned the
corner of the wall he saw that someone was ahead of him.
The figure was quite unmistakable — Doctor Tokareff
was hurrying down the little path into the thicket.

On an impulse Nigel drew back into a low doorway in
the wall. He felt quite incapable of listening just then to
any more of the Russian's heated dissertations about the
infamy of English police methods, and thought he would
give him time to get well away. It was only after a minute
or so had passed that Nigel began to wonder what
Tokareff was up to. There has been something odd about
his manner, a kind of light furtiveness; and what had he

been carrying? Laughing a little to himself, Nigel made up his mind to wait until the Russian returned. He vaulted over the locked gate and settled himself down with his back against the sun-warmed brick of the orchard wall. A puckered apple lay in the withered grass where he sat. He bit into the soft flesh of it. It tasted floury and sweetly stale.

He must have waited there for ten minutes and was beginning to get sick of it, when again he heard the light, firm step, and drawing back against the wall, caught a momentary glimpse of Tokareff hurrying back up the path. He was not carrying anything.

'Money for jam,' said Nigel to himself, and waited another two minutes, and then returned to the path following down into the thicket.

He had not gone very far before he came to the source of the blue smoke. A little fire, such as gardeners build from underbrush and damp leaves, was smouldering in a clearing. Nigel examined it closely. It looked as though someone had been raking it over, and it now smelt less pleasantly. He pushed the top layer of smoking rubbish on one side, and there, sure enough, was a solid wedge of crisp note-paper, already half-burnt away.

'Crikey!' ejaculated Nigel, snatching a page from the burning and examining it excitedly. It was covered in ridiculous pen-and-ink marks that he felt every justification in calling Russian. He drew in his breath, and was instantly choked with smoke. Gasping and spluttering and burning his fingers, he dragged out the rest of the paper and danced on it. His eyes streamed, and he coughed insufferably.

'Are you keen on war dances, Mr Bathgate?' said a voice beyond the smoke.

'Hell's boots!' panted Nigel, and sat down on the trophy.

Inspector Alleyn bore down on him through the smoke.

'Two minds with but a single thought,' he said politely. 'I was just going to try a little rescue work myself.'

Nigel was speechless, but he got off the papers.

Alleyn picked them up and looked them over.

'These are old acquaintances,' he said, 'but I think we'll keep them this time. Thank you very much, Mr Bathgate.'

CHAPTER 10

Black Fur

To the members of the house-party at Frantock the days before the inquest seemed to have avoided the dimensions of time and slipped into eternity.

Alleyn refused Sir Hubert's offer of a room, and was believed to be staying at the Frantock Arms in the village. He appeared at different times and in different places, always with an air of faint preoccupation, unvaryingly courteous, completely remote. Rosamund Grant was reported by Doctor Young to be suffering from severe nervous shock, and still kept her room. Mrs Wilde was querulous and inclined to be hysterical. Arthur Wilde spent most of his time answering her questions and listening to her complaints and running useless errands for her. Tokareff drove them all demented with his vehement expostulations, and seriously annoyed Angela by suddenly developing a tendency to make comic-opera love to her. 'He is mad, of course,' she said to Nigel on Wednesday morning in the library. 'Imagine it! A flirtation with a charge of murder hanging over all our heads.'

'All Russians seem a bit dotty to me,' rejoined Nigel. 'Look at Vassily. Do you think now that he did it?'

'I'm certain he didn't. The servants say he was in and

out of the pantry the whole time, and Roberts, the other man, says he was speaking to Vassily in there two minutes before the gong sounded.'

'Then why did he do a bolt?'

'Nerves, I should think,' said Angela thoughtfully. 'Uncle Hubert says all Russians of Vassily's age and class are terrified of the police.'

'The others all think he did it,' Nigel ventured.

'Yes, and Marjorie says so about forty times a day. Oh dear, how short-tempered I'm getting!'

'You're a—a wonder,' finished Nigel nervously.

'Don't you start!' said Miss North cryptically. She was silent for a moment, and then burst out suddenly: 'Oh poor Charles! poor old Charles—it's so horrible to be thankful they've taken him away. We were always so sorry when he went,' and, for the first time since the tragedy, she burst into a fit of uncontrollable sobbing.

Nigel ached to put his arms round her. He stood above her muttering, 'Angela dear. Please, Angela—'

She held out a hand to him gropingly, and he took it and rubbed it between both of his. A voice sounded in the hall outside, and Angela sprang to her feet and ran out of the room.

Following her, Nigel bumped into Alleyn in the hall.

'Wait a second,' said the detective. 'I wanted to see you. Come into the library.'

Nigel hesitated, and then followed him.

'What's the matter with Miss North?' asked Alleyn.

'What's the matter with all of us?' rejoined Nigel. 'It's enough to drive anyone dippy.'

'It's a pity about you!' commented Alleyn tartly. 'How would you like to be a detective, the lousiest job in creation?'

'I wouldn't mind changing with you,' said Nigel.

'Wouldn't you, then! Well, you can have a stab at it since you're so eager. Every sleuth ought to have a tame halfwit, to make him feel clever. I offer you the job, Mr Bathgate — no salary, but a percentage of the honour and glory.'

'You're very good,' said Nigel, who never knew quite where he was with Alleyn. 'Am I to conclude I have been degummed from the list of suspects?'

'Oh, yes,' groaned the detective wearily. 'You're cleared. Ethel the Intelligent spoke to you half a second before the lights went out.'

'Who is Ethel the Intelligent?'

'The second housemaid.'

'Oh, yes,' cried Nigel. 'I remember; she was actually there when the lights went out. I'd quite forgotten her.'

'Well, you are a bright lad. A pretty girl establishes your alibi for you, and you forget all about her.'

'I suppose Mr and Mrs Wilde are safe enough, too?' said Nigel.

'See Florence the Farsighted. You do, do you? Shall we take a stroll to the gate?'

'If you like. A gentleman in a mackintosh will be there pretending to botanize in the iron railings.'

'One of my myrmidons. Never mind, a walk will do you good.'

Nigel consented, and they went out into the thin sunshine.

'Mr Bathgate,' said Alleyn quietly, 'every single member of this household is concealing something from me. You are yourself, you know.'

'What do you mean?'

'Exactly what I say. Look here, I'm going to be frank with you. This murder was committed from inside the house. Roberts had the front door locked at six-thirty, a regular trick of his apparently, and anyway it had rained before six o'clock, was fine until eight, and after that there was a hard frost. Your crime books will have told you that under those conditions the gardens of the great are as an open book to us sleuths. The murderer was inside the house.'

'What about Vassily? Why hasn't he been caught?'

'He has been caught.'

'What!'

'Certainly, and released again. We managed to keep your brothers of the penny press quiet over that.'

'You say he didn't do it.'

'Do I?'

'Well, don't you?'

'I say you are all, each one of you, hiding something from me.'

Nigel was silent.

'It's a horrible affair,' continued Alleyn after a pause, 'but believe me you can do no good—no manner of good—by keeping me in the dark. Look here, Mr Bathgate, you are a poor actor. I saw you watching Mrs Wilde and Miss Grant. There's something there that hasn't come out, and I fancy you know what it is.'

'I—oh lord, Alleyn, it's all so beastly. Anyway, if I do know anything, it doesn't amount to a row of beans.'

'Forgive me, but you don't know in the least little bit what it may amount to. Had you met Mrs Wilde before you came here?'

'No.'

'Miss Grant?'

'Once—at my cousin's house.'

'Had your cousin ever talked to you about either of them?'

'Apart from casually mentioning them, never.'

'How far had this flirtation with Mrs Wilde gone?'

'I don't know—I mean—how do you know—?'

'He held her in his arms on Saturday night.'

Nigel felt and looked extremely uncomfortable.

'If he had her in his room,' said Alleyn brutally.

'It was not in his room,' said Nigel, and could have

bitten his tongue out.

'Ah! Then where was it? Come now, I've got under your guard. Better tell me.'

'How do you know he held her in his arms?'

'"You have just told me," said the great detective quietly,' quoted Alleyn. 'I know because his dinner-jacket was significantly stained with her liquid powder. Presumably it was clean when he arrived, and he had not changed on the night he was killed. Therefore, it was on Saturday night. Am I right?'

'I suppose so.'

'It must have been before dinner. When did you handle the Männlicher in the gun-room?'

'Oh, hell!' said Nigel. 'I'll come clean.'

He gave as sparse an account as he could of the duologue between Rankin and Mrs Wilde. By the time he had finished they had crossed the little footbridge in the wood and were in sight of the gates.

'You tell me,' said Alleyn, 'that after you had heard Rankin and Mrs Wilde leave the room and had entered it yourself, someone turned out the lights. Might that not have been Rankin himself returning to do so?'

'No,' said Nigel. 'I heard him shut the door and go away. No, it was someone who had sat at the far end of the drawing-room—beyond the "elbow" of the room, you know—and, like me, had overheard.'

'Have you any impression of them?'

'How could I?'

'It is possible. Their sex, for instance.'

'I—please don't attach any significance to this—I rather felt—why, I don't know—that it was a woman.'

'And here we are at the gates. Mr Alfred Bliss, he of the mackintosh, is, as you see, greatly interested in a distant view of an AA telephone box. We won't disturb him. My dear lad, let us embark on a little ramble.'

'Good lord, what do you mean—a ramble?'

'Have you never read *Eyes and No Eyes*? I am going to improve your keen young journalistic brain. Come on.'

He turned off the avenue into the woods, with Nigel at his heels. They followed the merest hint of a track that wound its way through dense undergrowth.

'I discovered this track,' said Alleyn, 'only yesterday. Acting on information received, as we say in the courts, I have come here to do a little genuine sleuthing. Someone came this way between four-thirty and six on Monday evening. I hope to learn something of their identity. Keep your eyes skinned, will you?'

Nigel tried to think of things that he ought to be looking for, and could arrive at nothing better than footprints and broken twigs. Alleyn walked very slowly, looking round him and down at the ground between each step. The ground was springy and quite dry. The wood smelt delicious, primal, and earthy. The track doubled and twisted. Alleyn turned his head this way and that, paused, squatted like a native, appeared to examine the ground between his feet, straightened up, and went slowly onwards.

Nigel stared at the intricate series of patterns made by green striking across green, and forgot to look for anything else. He wondered who had gone down this path before them, stirring the leaves, whose head had been darkly silhouetted against the patterns of green, whose presence had left the faint imprint which Alleyn so assiduously hunted.

Suddenly they were walking towards a high iron fence, and he realized that they had arrived at the edge of the wood where Frantock ran with the main road.

'Finis!' said Alleyn. 'End of the trail. Seen anything?'

'Afraid not.'

'Not much to see. Now look here. Look at these iron standards in the fence. Fairly well discoloured and stained, aren't they? Some sort of meagre little vegetable

has managed to make a living on them. Easily rubbed off,
though. Can you get your hand between them?'

'Not I.'

'Nor I neither. Someone managed to do it on Monday.
Look there—a small hand.' He leant his face down to the
rails and looked at them closely. Then cautiously he ran
his fingers down the stem, holding his handkerchief to
catch the minute fragments that fell into it. These in turn,
he scrutinized.

'Black fur,' he said, 'I *think* black fur.'

'Holmes, my dear fellow, this is supernatural,'
murmured Nigel.

'Holmes wasn't such a boob when all's said,' answered
Alleyn. 'Personally, I think those yarns are jolly clever.'

'As you say. Were you expecting to find black fur on
the railings, may I ask?'

'I hadn't hoped to—it's a help, of course.'

'For God's sake, Alleyn,' exploded Nigel, 'tell me a bit
more or don't tell me anything. I'm sorry, but I am rather
interested.'

'My dear fellow, I'm sorry, too. I assure you I'm not
being mysterious out of vanity or officiousness. If I told
you everything, every bit of evidence, every investigation
I think proper to make, you would suspect, as I have
suspected, every member of your house-party in turn. I
will tell you this much. On Monday, late in the afternoon,
a person whose identity I am anxious to establish came
here to this fence and, unseen by the waterproof at the
gates, threw a letter, stamped and addressed, out on to
the road there. It was picked up by a passing cyclist, who
took it into the village post office.'

'How did you nose all this out?'

'What an unattractive phrase that is! I didn't nose at
all. The cyclist, instead of putting the letter in the box,
handed it over the counter with a brief explanation of
where he had found it. The young woman in the basket

cuffs who guards His Majesty's mail in Little Frantock showed startling intelligence. I had, of course, asked her to stop all letters going out of Frantock and recognizing the locality, she thought there might be something up and held it back. It wasn't in a Frantock envelope either.'

'You have got it, then?'

'Yes, I will show it to you when we get back.'

'Is it illuminating?'

'Quite the reverse at present. But indirectly I hope it will be. Come on.'

They made their way out of the wood and tramped in silence back to Frantock. Nigel made but one remark. 'This time tomorrow,' he said, 'the inquest will be over.'

'Presumably—or adjourned.'

'Thank heaven for that, anyhow; we can at least go home.'

They walked up the steps to the front door.

'Come into the study for a moment,' invited Alleyn.

The study had been set apart as a sort of private office for him. He unlocked the door, and Nigel followed him in.

'Light the fire, will you?' said Alleyn; 'we shall be some time.'

Nigel lit the fire and his pipe, and settled himself down in the armchair.

'Here is the letter,' said Alleyn. From his breast pocket he produced a white envelope, and handed it to Nigel.

'I may tell you,' he said, 'that there were no finger-prints on it; of course, I have by this time got photos of all your fingerprints.'

'Oh, quite,' said Nigel rather blankly.

The envelope bore a typed adress:

Miss Sandilands
P.O. Shamperworth St
Dulwich

The enclosure was also typed; on a piece of the green note-paper used by Sir Hubert and distributed throughout all the bedrooms. Nigel read it aloud.

'Please destroy the parcel in Tunbridge B. at once and do not tell a soul.'

There was no signature.

'The envelope,' said Alleyn, 'tells us nothing—it came from an odd packet of white stationery in the library writing-desk.'

'And the type?'

'Corresponds with the machine in the library, which also yields no fingerprints except the housemaid's, and a few very blurred and ancient ones left by Sir Hubert. This letter was typed by an inexperienced person—there are several mistakes, as you see.'

'Have you traced the female—Miss Sandilands?'

'A CID man went to the post office in Shamperworth Street yesterday. A clerk there remembered a woman calling in the morning to ask if there were any letters for Miss Sandilands. There was none, and she has not been in since then.'

'She may go again.'

'Certainly, but I don't want to wait.'

'What do you propose to do? Run up and down Tunbridge looking for a parcel?'

'I see you are in merry pin. No, I propose to work from this end, and with the aid of my bits of black fur, it ought not to be difficult.'

'And the fur?'

Alleyn produced from his pocket his inevitable and rather insignificant Woolworth note-book.

'Meet my brain,' he said, 'without it I'm done.' He turned the leaves rapidly, muttering to himself.

'Personnel. Details of characters. Hobbies. Here we are—clothes. Clothes. Bathgate, Grant, Grant. Wearing at the time of incident—no. Chest of drawers, pink silk—

no. In wardrobe, that's more likely. Red leather coat, brown musquash, green and brown tweed coat and skirt. Red cap. Um—nothing there.'

'You have been very industrious,' said Nigel.

'My memory's so bad,' Alleyn apologized.

'Don't be affected,' said Nigel.

'Shut up. I hate your bedroom slippers and I know you use corn plaster. Handesley. Housemaids. North. Let's see.'

'Surely you are wasting your time making lists of Angela's underclothes,' said Nigel hotly.

'Don't be cross with me—I get no kick out of them. There's nothing there. Rankin. Tokareff—has *he* got a fur coat? Yes, he has, like an impresario's; still, his gloves are size eight. Try again. Wilde. Arthur, Mr and Mrs.' He stopped muttering, and a curiously blank look suddenly masked his face.

'Well?' asked Nigel.

Alleyn passed him the little note-book. In it, written in an incredibly fine upright hand, Nigel read:

'Wilde. Mrs Marjorie. Age about thirty-two. Height five foot four approx.' Here followed a detailed description of Marjorie Wilde, in which even the size of her gloves were noted. Then:

'Wardrobe. In hanging cupboard, Harris tweed coat and skirt, shepherd's plaid overcoat. Burberry raincoat, blue. Black astrakhan overcoat, black fur collar and cuffs.'

'Black fur collar and cuffs,' repeated Nigel aloud. 'Oh, lord!'

'Size in gloves, six and a quarter,' said Alleyn, and took the book. 'Where is Mrs Wilde at the moment, Bathgate?'

'She *was* in the library.'

'Go and see if she's still there, and come back and tell me.'

Nigel was away three minutes.

'They are all there,' he said; 'it's nearly teatime.'

'Then come upstairs after me and walk slowly to your own door. If you see anyone approaching, come through the bathroom into Wilde's dressing-room and warn me. I shall be in Mrs Wilde's room.'

He went out swiftly, and Nigel followed in time to see him running, cat-like, upstairs. By the time Nigel reached the landing the inspector had disappeared.

Nigel walked to his own door and paused, taking his cigarette case out and groping in his pockets for matches. His heart was beating thickly. Had he been standing there hours or seconds when he heard a light footstep coming from the long corridor? He struck a match as Florence appeared, strolled through his own door, and then darted swiftly into the bathroom.

'Alleyn!' he whispered urgently. 'Alleyn!' Then he stopped short, flabbergasted.

Arthur Wilde was washing his hands at the basin.

CHAPTER 11

Confession?

Nigel was so greatly taken aback that some seconds elapsed before he realized that Wilde was equally disconcerted. His face was extremely pale, and he stood very still, his hands plunged incongruously in the soapy water.

'I—I'm sorry,' stammered Nigel at last. 'I thought you were Alleyn.'

Wilde achieved a wan smile. 'Alleyn?' he said. 'Yes, so I gathered, Bathgate. Will you tell me, did you think Alleyn was here or—in my wife's room?'

Nigel was silent.

'I wish you could see your way to answering me,' said Wilde very quietly. He took a towel from the rack and began to dry his hands. Suddenly he dropped the towel on the floor and whispered, 'My God, this is a terrible business.'

'Terrible!' echoed Nigel helplessly.

'Bathgate,' said Wilde in a sudden gust of passion, 'you must tell me—did you expect to find the inspector here or behind that dressing-room door in Marjorie's room? Answer me.'

The door from the bathroom into the dressing-room was wide open, but the one beyond it was shut. Nigel looked involuntarily towards this door.

'I assure you—' he began.

'You are a bad liar, Bathgate,' said a voice from beyond. The door was opened, and Alleyn walked through.

'You were quite right, Mr Wilde,' said he. 'I have been carrying out a little investigation in your wife's room. I have done so in all your rooms, you know. It is essential.'

'You had already been through everything,' said Wilde. 'Why must you torture us like this? My wife has nothing—nothing to conceal. How could she have killed Rankin, and in that way? She has a horror of knives, an inhibition against them. Everyone knows that she can't touch a knife or a blade of any sort. Why, even on the night of this crime—Bathgate, you remember!—she got into a fever at the very sight of that filthy dagger. It's impossible, I tell you, it's impossible!'

'Mr Wilde, that is all I am trying to prove, that it is impossible.'

Something like a sob escaped the little man.

'Steady, Wilde,' said Nigel sheepishly.

'Will you hold your tongue, sir!' shouted the archaeologist. Involuntarily, Nigel had a swift mental picture of him turning on an unruly or impertinent student. 'I must ask you to forgive me, Bathgate,' he added immediately. 'I am not myself, indeed I am not.'

'Of course you are not,' said Nigel quickly; 'and remember Mrs Wilde has an alibi—a perfect alibi, surely. Florence, Angela's maid, and I myself both know she was in her room. Don't we, Alleyn?' He turned desperately to the detective. Alleyn did not answer.

There was a rather ghastly silence. Then abruptly:

'I think tea is waiting, Mr Wilde,' said the inspector. 'Bathgate, may I have a word with you downstairs before I go?'

Nigel followed him to the door, and they were about to go out when an exclamation from Wilde arrested them.

'Stop!'

They both turned.

Wilde was standing in the middle of the room, his hands were pressed tightly together, his face, raised a little, was yet in shadow since the window was behind him. He spoke slowly.

'Inspector Alleyn,' he said, 'I have decided to confess. I killed Rankin. I hoped that the necessity for this admission would not arise. But I can't bear the strain any longer—and now—my wife! I killed him.'

Alleyn said nothing. He and Wilde were looking fixedly at each other. Nigel had never seen a face so devoid of expression as the detective's.

'Well?' Wilde's voice was hysterical. 'Aren't you going to give me the usual warning? The customary cliché! Anything I say will be taken down and may be used in evidence against me?'

Nigel suddenly heard himself speaking. '. . . it's impossible—impossible,' he was saying. 'You were in your bath, there in that bath: I spoke to you, I know you were there. Good God, Wilde, you can't do this, you can't tell us . . . When—how did you do it?' He stopped appalled by the inadequacy of his own words. At last

Alleyn spoke.

'Yes,' he said gently; 'when did you do it, Mr Wilde?'

'Before I came upstairs. When I was alone with him.'

'What about Mary, the under-housemaid, who saw him alive after you had gone?'

'She—she made a mistake—she has forgotten, I was still there.'

'Then how did you manage to talk through this door to Mr Bathgate here?'

Wilde did not answer.

'You tell me,' said Alleyn, turning to Nigel, 'that you were talking to each other continuously before and while the lights were out?'

'Yes.'

'Yet, Mr Wilde, you turned the lights out, and then took the trouble to sound the gong, and thus warn the entire household you had committed murder.'

'It was the game. I—I didn't mean to kill him. I didn't realize . . .'

'You mean that while you were busily talking to Mr Bathgate upstairs, you were also in the hall where, under the nose of a housemaid who did not happen to notice, you struck Mr Rankin in fun with an exceedingly sharp dagger which you had previously had leisure to examine?'

Silence.

'Well, Mr Wilde?' said Alleyn compassionately.

'Don't you believe me?' cried Wilde.

'Frankly, no.' Alleyn opened the door. 'But you have been playing an extremely dangerous game. I shall be in the study for a minute or two, Bathgate.'

He went out shutting the door behind him. Wilde walked to the window and leant across the ledge. Suddenly he bent his head and buried his face in his arm. Nigel thought he had never before seen so tragic a figure.

'Look here,' he said swiftly, 'you've been letting your nerves get the better of you. I am certain no one suspects

your wife. Alleyn himself knows it is impossible. We three
—you, she and I—are on the face of it exempt. You've
told a brave lie, but a damn' silly one. Pull yourself
together and forget it.' He touched Wilde lightly on the
shoulder and left him.

Alleyn was waiting for him downstairs.

'I plucked up my courage and asked Miss Angela if we
three might have tea together in here,' said the inspector.
'She is bringing it in herself, as I thought it unnecessary to
bother the servants.'

'Really?' Nigel wondered what was afoot now. 'What
an extraordinary incident that was just now.'

'Very.'

'I suppose it is not unusual for highly-strung people to
do that sort of thing—I did it myself.'

'So you did, but Wilde had a better reason, poor devil.'

'I admired him for it.'

'So did I, enormously.'

'Of course, his wife is innocent?'

Alleyn did not answer.

'Look at her alibi,' said Nigel.

'Yes,' said Allen, 'I'm looking at it. It's a lovely alibi,
isn't it?'

Angela came in with the tea.

'Well, Mr Alleyn,' she said, setting the tray on a stool
before the fire, 'what are you up to now?'

'Sit down, Miss Angela,' invited Alleyn, 'and give us
some tea if you please. Very strong and no milk for me.
Do you know anyone called Sandilands?'

Angela paused, cup in hand.

'Sandilands? N-no, I don't think so. Wait a moment,
though. Is that strong enough?'

'Thank you so much. Perfect.'

'Sandilands?' repeated Angela meditatively. 'Yes, now
I *do*. Where have I met—?'

'Was it at—?' began Nigel.

'Take your tea and be tacit,' advised Alleyn curtly.

Nigel glared at him and was silent.

'I've got it,' said Angela. 'There's an old Miss Sandi-lands, a sewing-maid. She sometimes does work for Marjorie.'

'That's the one,' said Alleyn brightly; 'she worked for them at Tunbridge, didn't she?'

'At Tunbridge? The Wildes were never at Tunbridge.'

'Perhaps Mrs Wilde stays there—visits there—takes a cure there? I may have got muddled.'

'I never heard of it,' said Angela decisively. 'Marjorie is not at all like Tunbridge.'

'Oh, well, never mind,' rejoined the inspector. 'Has Miss Grant told you where she was while you were bathing on Sunday evening?'

Angela looked gravely at him and then turned to Nigel.

'Oh, Nigel,' she said, 'what is he thinking?'

'Search me,' said Nigel gloomily.

'Please, Miss Angela?' said Alleyn.

'She hasn't *told* me. But—oh, am I right to go on?'

'Indeed, indeed you are.'

'Then—I believe . . . I think I know where she went.' Yes?'

'To Charles's room!'

'What makes you think that?'

'The morning afterwards you asked me to have his room locked and to give you the key. I went to do it myself. Rosamund has a pair of bath slippers—mules, you know—'

'Yes, yes, with green fluffy stuff, marabout or something, above the instep.'

'Yes,' agreed the astonished Angela. 'Well, the key was on the inside, so I had to enter the room to get it. I saw a wisp of the green fluff on the carpet.'

'Madam!' said Alleyn triumphantly, 'you are superb. And you picked up the bit of green fluff and—? You didn't throw it away?'

'I didn't, but I will if you are going to use it against Rosamund.'

'Here! Oi! No blackmailing, please. You kept it because you thought it might save her. That it?'

'Yes.'

'Well. Hang on to it. Now tell me this. What was the relationship between Rankin and Miss Grant?'

'I can't discuss anything of that sort,' said Angela coldly.

'My dear child, this is no time for coming over all county with me. I quite appreciate your scruples, but they are not worth much when they are used to screen a murderer or to cast suspicion on an innocent person. I shouldn't ask you unless I had to. Let me tell you what I think. There was an understanding between Rankin and Miss Grant. He wanted her to marry him. She had refused because of his relationship with another woman. Am I right?'

'Yes, I'm afraid so.'

'Was she fond of him?'

'Yes.'

'That was what I wanted to know. Was she jealous?'

'No, no! Not jealous, but she—she felt it very deeply indeed.'

Alleyn opened his note-book again, and drew out a fragment of blotting-paper and passed it to Angela. 'Take your handglass and look at that,' he said.

Angela obeyed him, and then passed the blotting-paper and mirror to Nigel. He read without difficulty:

'October 10th: Dear Joyce, I'm sorry to muddle your pl . . .'

'Whose writing is that?' asked Alleyn.

'It is Rosamund's,' said Angela.

'It was written after seven-thirty on Saturday night at the desk in the elbow of the drawing-room,' commented the inspector, looked at Nigel. 'At seven-thirty the excellent Ethel had tidied the desk and put out fresh blotting-paper. On Sunday morning, noticing the stains on this sheet, she turned it under, putting a clean sheet on top.'

'So you imagine—?' Nigel began.

'I do not imagine; detectives aren't allowed to imagine. They note probabilities. I am firmly of the opinion that Miss Grant overheard, with you, the duologue between Mrs Wilde and Rankin. It was she who turned out the lights and nipped out ahead of you on your leaving the drawing-room.'

'I'm quite at sea,' complained Angela.

Nigel told her briefly of the conversation he had overheard from the gun-room. Angela was silent for a few minutes. Then she turned to Alleyn.

'There is one factor in this case,' she began in a quaintly pedantic manner, 'that puzzles me above all others.'

'Will my learned friend propound?' asked Alleyn solemnly.

'I am about to do so. Why, oh why, did the murderer sound the gong? I can understand his turning out the lights. He knew that in doing so, by the rules of the murder game, he ensured himself a clear two minutes to get away. But why, oh why, did he bang the gong?'

'To keep up the illusion of the game?' Nigel speculated.

'It seems so incredible somehow—to make a proclamatory gesture like that. Darkness he would welcome, yes, but to start that clamour—it sounds so—so psychologically unsound.'

'My learned friend's point is well urged,' said Alleyn. 'But I put it to her that the murderer or murderess did not sound the gong.'

'Then,' said Nigel and Angela together, 'who did?'

'Rankin.'

'What!' they shouted.

'Rankin sounded the gong.'

'What the devil do you mean?' ejaculated Nigel.

'I'm not going to give all my tricks away, and this is such a very simple one that you ought to have seen it yourselves.' Nigel and Angela merely stared blankly at each other.

'Well, we don't,' said Nigel flatly.

'Later perhaps it may dawn,' commented the detective. 'In the meantime, how about a run up to London tonight?'

'To London—what for?'

'I hear that you, Miss Angela, are the fastest thing known off the dirt track, and when I use the expression "the fastest thing" I use it literally, not colloquially. Will you, without explaining your movements to anyone, drive this young ornament of the Press up to London in the Bentley and do a job of work for me? I will talk to your uncle about it for you.'

'Now—tonight?' said Angela.

'It is getting dark. I think you may start in half an hour. You *must* be back here when it gets light tomorrow morning, but I hope you may return long before dawn. On second thoughts I think I shall accompany you.'

He looked, apparently in some amusement, at the not conspicuously delighted faces of the other two.

'I shall sleep in the back seat,' he added vaguely. 'I've had too many late nights.'

'Will you come, Nigel?' Angela asked.

'Of course I will,' said Nigel. 'What are we to do when we get there?'

'If you will give me the pleasure of dining with me, both of you, I will explain myself then. Now, just one more question: you heard Mr Rankin's story of how he became possessed of the knife with which he was killed. Can either of you remember anything, anything at all,

that Rankin said which would serve to describe the man
who gave it to him?'

'What *did* Charles say, Nigel?' asked Angela after a
pause.

Alleyn crossed to the windows and stood by the drawn
curtains. He looked singularly alert.

'He told us,' said Nigel thoughtfully, 'that a Russian
whom he met in Switzerland gave it to him. He said it had
been sent to him. It was in return for some service Charles
did this Russian.'

'And that was?' Alleyn moved back into the room.

'I think he said something about pulling him out of a
crevasse.'

'That's all?'

'I can't remember anything else, can you, Angela?'

'I'm trying to think,' murmured Angela.

'Did you gather that they had become friends? Did
Rankin describe the man?'

'No,' said Nigel.

'N-no, but he said *something* else,' Angela asserted.

'What could it have been? Think now. Was it something about the accident that led to this incident? Were
either of them injured? What!' Angela had uttered a short
exclamation.

'That's it! The Russian lost two of his fingers with
frostbite.'

'The devil he did!' ejaculated Alleyn. 'The devil he
did!'

'Is that relevant?' asked Nigel.

'It is extremely important,' said Alleyn very loudly. 'It
links up the Russian evidence very prettily. Let me just
explain precisely what I mean by the Russian evidence.'
While he was speaking the detective had risen and was
standing facing the other two with his back to the
curtained windows. The lamplight fell strongly on his
dark head and broad shoulders. 'Let me tell you,' he said

emphatically, 'that on Saturday night a Pole was murdered in Soho. He was identified by his left hand.' Alleyn slowly raised his own left arm under the lamp and spread the thumb, index and little fingers of the hand. The two middle fingers he doubled over the palm.

For perhaps two seconds Nigel and Angela sat staring at him in silence. Then they realized that he was whispering urgently, his hand was still raised.

'Bathgate!' he was murmuring, 'Tokareff is outside watching us. In one minute I shall turn and make for the french window. Follow me and help me collar him. You, Miss Angela, go out of the door as if nothing had happened, speak to no one. Wrap yourself up quickly in the first coat you can find and wait for us in the Bentley.' Then aloud, and lowering his arm as Angela left the room, he added, 'And now we are alone, Bathgate, let me tell you exactly what I know of these Russians . . .'

He had whirled round and was at the french window before Nigel had got to his feet. The curtain was torn aside violently; Alleyn wrenched at the door.

'Blast!' he said. 'Come on!'

There was a crash of splintered glass, a cold wind filled the warm room. Alleyn disappeared with Nigel close on his heels.

CHAPTER 12

An Arrest and a Night Journey

Outside on the frozen balcony two men struggled together bitterly and silently. The uncertain lamplight, broken by the billowing curtains, wavered across them. Nigel had a swift glimpse of Tokareff's face, spectacled, strangely passive. He flung himself at the Russian, tackling him low, and was himself bowled over, striking his face against the icy, frost-smelling stones. A moment later he saw Alleyn stagger backwards, and as he himself scrambled up he was aware of a figure that melted away out into the dark.

'After him!' Alleyn grunted. A shrill whistle split the night air.

Nigel was running across the lawn, vaguely conscious of the rush of cold air on his eyes and lips. 'The wood!' he thought, 'he mustn't reach the wood.' He could hear the dull rhythm of the Russian's feet of the soft turf. With a stringent effort he quickened his pace, sprinted and then dived, bringing the unseen fugitive down with him.

'This is better,' thought Nigel, wrenching a wrist and arm across a writhing back, 'I've got him.'

'Got him!' echoed Alleyn's voice out of the darkness, and in a moment the detective knelt beside him, and a bull's-eye lantern heralded the approach at the double of Bunce, PC.

Tokareff uttered a short, gasping sound, a sort of groan.

'Now then,' said Alleyn, 'let's have my torch.'

A pencil of light shot out. Tokareff lay on his back with Alleyn sitting across him.

'Get back to your post, Bunce, as quick as you can,' the detective ordered sharply. 'Is Green still there?'

'Yessir,' breathed Bunce; 'we heard your whistle.'

'Miss North, Mr Bathgate, and I will come through in the Bentley in ten minutes. Have the gates open and don't stop us. Keep a cat's own watch for anything else. Now skedaddle!'

'Yessir,' blew Bunce in the dark, and the bull's-eye retired.

'Now then, Doctor Tokareff. There's a perfectly good revolver cuddled into your ribs here, and I think you will come quietly.'

'*Proklyatie! proklyatie!*' stuttered a furious voice. Something clicked sharply.

'Yes, I dare say. Come now, get up.'

The three stood facing each other in the darkness to which their eyes had grown accustomed.

'I don't think he carries any deadly weapings,' said Alleyn; 'but have a look, will you, Bathgate? Doctor Tokareff, you must consider yourself under arrest. Nothing in his hip pocket, or anywhere? Sure? Right. Now this way quickly. Damn, too late! Here's the hue and cry. Oh, well, no matter.'

The sound of voices drifted across from the house. Two figures were silhouetted against the dishevelled warmth of the study windows.

'Alleyn! Bathgate!' called Sir Hubert.

'Here we are!' answered Alleyn. 'Nothing's the matter.'

'Nozzing ze matter!' bellowed the suddenly articulate Russian. 'I greatly beg a difference. I am under an arrest. I am innocent of this murder! Sir Hubert! Mr Ooilde!'

'Come one,' said Alleyn, and he and Nigel propelled their captive back towards the house.

Handesley and Wilde met them in the pool of light outside the windows.

'Just a little Russian touch,' explained Alleyn. 'Manacles at midnight. A home away from home for the doctor.'

'Doctor Tokareff,' said Sir Hubert, 'this is a terrible business.'

'Tokareff!' murmured Wilde to Nigel. 'Tokareff, after all!' And Nigel wondered if there had crept into his voice a note of exquisite relief or only one of profound astonishment. The Russian was protesting vehemently, his manacled hands clasped in front of his face. Nigel felt an insane desire to giggle.

'Sir Hubert,' Alleyn continued, exactly as if the

Russian was not speaking, 'please do you and Mr Wilde return indoors. You may explain briefly to the others what has happened.

'What are you going to do?'

'We shall be away for some time. I shall get Miss Angela to drive us to the local police station. Doctor Tokareff—'

'I am innocent! Ask the peasant Vassily, the butler! He knows—on the night of the crime—I must tell you.'

'I have to warn you,' interrupted Alleyn, and Nigel saw him glance inimically at Wilde, 'that anything you say will be taken down and may be used in evidence against you. Later on, if you choose, you can make a statement. Now, Sir Hubert, and you too, Mr Wilde, please go in. I shall communicate with you later.' The others turned silently towards the house.

'Lawyers!' roared Tokareff after them. 'Lawyers! judges! magistrates! How you call them? I must have them of the best.'

'So you shall. Bless the boy. Come on,' said Alleyn, as the others disappeared. 'Come on, Bathgate, round the house to the garage, and, Doctor Tokareff, I really must insist—no more *Deaths of Boris*.'

He led them without hesitation to the back drive, where in a softly palpitating Bentley they found Angela.

'Good girl!' said Alleyn softly. 'Doctor Tokareff will come with us, as you see. In you get, Doctor. Bathgate, you sit in front. To the local quod, please, miss.'

'Streuth!' whispered Angela, as the Bentley ate up the drive.

'Streuth indeed!' agreed Nigel. 'Tokareff is under arrest.'

'For the murder?'

'For what else?'

'But—he sang the *Death of Boris* all the time.'

'Seems he couldn't have.'

'Well, here we are,' commented Angela after an indecently brief interval. She slowed down and put on her brakes.

'Will you wait for us?' Alleyn asked her. 'Come on, Doctor Tokareff.'

A police sergeant showed them into a brilliantly lit, white-washed room. A tall blue-uniformed officer greeted them.

'Inspector Fisher—Mr Bathgate,' said Alleyn by way of introduction. 'This is Doctor Tokareff. I wish to charge him with—'

Tokareff, who had been perfectly silent for some time, broke in. 'I am innocent of murder!'

'Who said you weren't?' rejoined Alleyn wearily. 'The charge is one of sedition and conspiracy, if that's the correct phrase. I always get them wrong, don't I, Fisher? This man is charged with complicity in connection with the operations of an association of Russians having its headquarters at 101 Little Racquet Street, Soho. He is charged with having caused to be published and circulated certain pamphlets containing treasonable utterances and incitements to sedition and—oh, damn it, anyway, that's the charge.'

'Righto,' said Inspector Fisher, crossing to a desk and putting on his spectacles. 'Let's have it.'

A brief colloquy between the two policemen followed, interspersed by the scratching of the inspector's pen. The sergeant came in and said cheerfully: 'Now then, Doctor, we'll just move next door.'

'I wish to write, to make an announcement,' said Doctor Tokareff suddenly.

'You shall have every opportunity,' soothed Alleyn. 'What a tig you are in, to be sure!'

'It is the knife,' said Tokareff profoundly. 'The betrayal of the knife that has been to me my own betrayal. The Pole, Krasinski, who gave it to Mr Rankin was the author of all these misfortunates.'

'Krasinski is dead,' said Alleyn, 'and letters of yours were in his pockets. Who killed him?'

'How should I know? In the brotherhood no one knows. Krasinski was mad. I wish to write to my country's ambassador.'

'You may do so. He'll be delighted. We'll leave you now, Fisher. I'll ring through at about one o'clock. Good night.'

'Good night,' mumbled Nigel uncomfortably, and followed the detective out to the car.

Angela did nothing to darken her reputation as a furious driver on that night trip to London. Alleyn refused to talk after having given an address off Coventry Street as their destination, and slept deeply on the back seat. Nigel stared at a young, eager profile and thought his own thoughts.

'Do you think Mr Alleyn believes Doctor Tokareff did it?' she said.

'I don't know a bit,' Nigel answered her. 'As far as I can make it out, Tokareff, perhaps Vassily your butler, and the Pole Krasinski whom Charles met in Switzerland, must all have been members of some Bolshie gang. Krasinski, God knows why, gave Charles Rankin the knife. I guess, from what Sir Hubert, Arthur Wilde, and Tokareff himself have said, that the knife was the symbolic weapon of the brotherhood, and to part with it was a fatal breach of trust. So, on Saturday evening somebody murdered Krasinski in Soho.'

'And on Sunday someone murdered Charles Rankin at Frantock,' concluded Angela under her breath. 'Do you think Tokareff could have darted out of his bedroom, rushed to the head of the stairs, thrown the knife, run back and gone on gaily with the *Death of Boris*?'

'Hardly. And who put out the lights?' objected Nigel.

'And what does Mr Alleyn mean by saying Charles

himself sounded the gong?' Angela ended hopelessly.

'I can't imagine, but I'm glad he's asleep. Angela, if I were to kiss the fur on your collar, would you mind very much?'

'We are now doing sixty, and we are going up to sixty-five. Is this a time for dalliance?'

'It may be my death,' said Nigel, 'but I'll risk it.'

'That wasn't the fur on my collar.'

'Darling!'

'What's the time?' said Alleyn suddenly from the back seat.

'We'll be there in twenty minutes,' called Angela, and was true to her words.

At the top of one of those curious little cul-de-sacs off Coventry Street, where the Bentley looked the size of a caravan, Alleyn fitted a latch-key into a green door.

'You will find that you know my servant,' he said over his shoulder.

And, sure enough, there in the little hall waiting for them was an elderly, apologetic figure, anxiously bent forward.

'Vassily!' cried Angela.

'Miss Angela, my little miss! *Dushitchka!*' The old Russian was covering her hands with kisses . . .

'Oh, Vassily!' said Angela gently, 'what have you to do with this? Why did you run away?'

'I was in terror. In such terrible fright. Picture, little miss, what would they think? I said to myself, the police will find out all. They will question Alexis Andreyevitch, Doctor Tokareff, and he will tell them perhaps that I also was of the brotherhood long, long ago in my own country. He will repeat what I have said: that Mr Rankin should not have the holy little knife that had been blessed to the bratsvo, the brothership. The English police, they know everything, and perhaps they already have known how I have had letters from the brotherhood in London. It will be useless for me to say that I am no longer, how you say, mixed up with this society. I am already suspect. So before the police come, I run away and am arrested here in London, and to Scotland Yard I have made my statement and to Inspector Alleyn when he comes up to see me on Sunday, and they release me and I stay here. It is splendid!'

'He behaved like an old donkey,' said Alleyn. 'Did you get my message, Vassily?'

'Yes, certainly, and already dinner is waiting and corktails.'

'Then let Miss Angela powder her nose in the guest suite, while Mr Bathgate and I remove the turf from our ears in the lonely west wing.'

Alleyn was still about this business when Nigel, emerging from a diminutive dressing-room, found Angela already in the inspector's extremely comfortable study.

'Tell me,' she said in an engaging whisper, 'do detective chief inspectors usually invite the relatives and friends of the victim to dine in their flat, and do they invariably engage disappearing butlers as their own servants as soon as they are freed from arrest?'

'Perhaps it is The Thing Done in the Yard,' answered Nigel; 'though, I must say, he doesn't conform to my mental pictures of a sleuth-hound. I had an idea they lived privately amidst inlaid linoleum, aspidistras, and enlarged photographs of constabulary groups.'

'Taking a strong cuppa at six-thirty in their shirt sleeves. Well, pooh to us for a couple of snobs, anyway.'

'All the same,' said Nigel, 'I do think he's a bit unorthodox. He must be a gent with private means who sleuths for sleuthing's sake.'

'Sorry to keep you waiting,' said Alleyn in the doorway. 'Have one of Vassily's "corktails", and then let us dine.'

Vassily, important and beaming, rolled back sliding

doors, and the inspector ushered them into the dining-room. The dinner was a very pleasant little ceremony. When Vassily had brought in coffee, set a decanter in front of the inspector, and taken himself off, Alleyn looked at his watch.

'We can talk for fifteen minutes,' he said, 'and then I want you to do a job of work for me. Perhaps I should say I can talk for fifteen minutes because I should like, if it wouldn't bore you, to go over the history of this case. It is of enormous help, I find, to talk to someone who is not a CID man. You needn't look so inordinately perky, Bathgate. I don't expect you to solve the mystery; I merely want you to tell me how clever I am, whether you think so or not.'

'Oke,' said Nigel tractably.

Alleyn gave him a friendly grin, lit a cigarette, and with a faintly didactic air began his *résumé*.

'I shall return to the official manner,' he said. 'I find it impresses you. Rankin was stabbed in the back at five minutes to eight. That was the time by your watch when the gong sounded, and your watch synchronized with Mary's, who told Wilde it was ten-to as he went upstairs. She saw him go up. You spoke to him when he went into the bathroom and during the time that followed; that leaves four minutes when Rankin was alone until the murder took place—less, because Mary didn't go away immediately. He was stabbed from behind, either by somebody over six feet, or by somebody standing on a raised area. In falling back he struck the gong with his head.'

'Oh!' gasped Angela and Nigel together.

'Yes, indeed. You were slow there. Baby-class stuff at the Yard, I do assure you. There was a very slight abrasion on the head, and I am pretty sure that was how it was caused. You all described the sound as a single, slightly muffled, booming note. "Skulls and brass in musical conjunction'', said I to myself. The moving of the body was definitely naughty—I was very cross about it—but that is how I reconstruct it. Rankin was bending over pouring out his drink, poor chap! The shaker was beside him on the floor and the glass overturned. Miss Grant noticed that. The murderer—I shan't bother to add "or murderess" every time—then switched off the lights, wearing a glove or having something wrapped round the hand. He then ran away. Where to? For reasons that I shan't bore you with, I think he went upstairs.

'Now, at that precise moment where was everybody? The servants are all accounted for, even that old goat Vassily, who was alone in the boot-room. You, Bathgate, were in your room. A housemaid saw you there when the gong sounded, and I have other excellent reasons for believing your evidence. Sir Hubert says he was in his dressing-room. You saw him there, Miss Angela, when you fetched the aspirin, and you had only just got back to Miss Grant's room when the alarm sounded. Sir Hubert is a very active man for his age, but he could not have got downstairs in that time, be he ever so nippy. You might possibly have managed it, but in your case, Miss Angela, there is a complete absence of motive and I have washed you out as a possibility. No *cause célèbre* for you this time.'

'Too kind,' muttered Nigel.

'Besides, Florence saw you in the passage. 'Saved by the Servants' is the subtitle as far as you two are concerned. Miss Grant went upstairs, bathed, went to Rankin's room, returned, found Florence in her room. Miss Grant, in her account, deliberately gave a miss to her visit to Rankin's room, but unless she had bribed Florence to tell a tarradiddle for her, their meeting, although it does not save her from coming definitely under suspicion, gives her a very short time in which to get downstairs, take the dagger from the wall, drive it home, and return. She studied medicine at the university, clever girl, and intended to become a doctor. Please don't interrupt, either of you.

'Tokareff sang in his bedroom, and Florence tells me she heard him. So did Sir Hubert. They are under the impression he was rendering the bellows of Boris unceasingly until the gong sounded. Such impressions are not very trustworthy. He may well have stopped for four minutes without their having any recollection of it.

'Mrs Wilde, whose room is at the head of the stairs, was nearest to the victim. You say you heard her talking after the lights went out. There are certain other features that go far towards scratching her off the list of possibles, but she has subsequently done one or two things that show she was desperately anxious to conceal certain aspects of her friendship for Rankin.'

'Surely,' ventured Angela gently, 'that is very understandable.'

'I think so too, but all the same, they must be cleared up. That is why you are going to help me tonight. Wilde we have dealt with exhaustively. We are all sick of Wilde. He has tried to give himself up for the murder, but his movements have been described from the time he left Rankin and went upstairs under the gaze of the housemaid until the gong sounded. Bathgate talked to him all the time, and Florence heard them. The bath gave an excellent fingerprint, and so on, and so on. He also left some prints on the banister, just to make it more difficult.

'Lastly, there is the melodramatic Russian element. Your uncle has written several excellent essays on Russian characteristics and customs. In my opinion, the truest thing he ever wrote about Russians was that no Englishman could understand them. The idea of a villainous secret brotherhood belongs to Merejkowski and contributors to *Chums*. The idea of Russians stabbing people in England because someone has given away a sacred dagger is so highly coloured that a decent policeman blushes to advance it. Yet Krasinski the Pole was murdered for this reason, Rankin was the man to whom the knife was given, and two members of the association were in the house when it happened. One is already under arrest for sedition, but—blast his eyes!— he sang while the murder was going on.'

'That,' said Angela mildly, 'establishes a beautiful alibi, doesn't it?'

'A bit too beautiful, you think, observed Alleyn appreciatively. 'Sagacious woman, you have stolen my stock bit of thunder. Yet sing he did, and—unless, as I have said, he *did* pause without anyone noticing the sudden lull, or unless he's a ventriloquist and threw the *Death of Boris* upstairs and along the back corridor—it's a teaser to get rid of. Well, here we are again. Let me say finally that there were no fingerprints on the dagger or on the strap from which it was taken, only Bathgate's prints on the electric switch and a muck-up of everybody's on the banister. Talking of the banister, Miss Angela, do you ever slide down it?'

'Yes—often,' said Angela, startled. 'We have competitions, face first without hanging on.'

'You did this on Saturday, perhaps?'

'No.'

'Can you go down face first? It's a bit tricky.'

'I can. Marjorie can't, and Doctor Tokareff was hopeless when we did it last weekend.'

'Look here!' shouted Nigel suddenly, 'what about Mary?'

'Mystery solved,' said Alleyn. 'Shall we go to a cinema, or would you rather return immediately?'

'Don't mock me,' insisted Nigel. 'Mary was the last to see him. She could have done it. And what was she doing in the front of the house? She's a tweeny. Her place is the back stairs. Look for the motive.'

'I shall. Meanwhile, I want Miss Angela to look for

something else. She is going to the Wildes' house in
Green Street. I want you, Miss Angela, to go in and
pretend to be a good deal sillier than you really are.'

'I suppose you mean to be nice,' said Angela. 'Who do
I ask for in my silly way?'

'You ask whoever comes to the door—will it be a maid
or a butler?—if they know where Sandilands is. You say
you are in London unexpectedly, and Mrs Wilde asked
you to call.'

'Now listen,' began Angela rebelliously.

'It's no good,' Alleyn interrupted, 'raising schoolgirl
scruples. When you do this job you will be helping to clear
an innocent person, if she is, as you seem to believe,
innocent. Well?'

'Go on, please.'

'You are to say you are simply too stupid for words and
cannot remember the message, but it was something Mrs
Wilde wanted, and you think Sandilands the sewing-maid
has it or knows where it is. You may say—yes, I think
you may say—it is a letter or some letters. Shake your
curls.'

'Revolting,' murmured Angela.

'Be vague and fashionable and "charming to the
servant" all at once. Murmur something about
Tunbridge, and ask if they can help.'

'About Tunbridge?'

Alleyn told her of the intercepted letter. To his astonishment Angela burst out laughing.

'My poor pet,' gasped Angela annoyingly, 'and did
you think you ought to go to Tunbridge, and were you all
muddledy-puddledy?'

'Miss Angela,' said Alleyn, 'it is not fitting that you
should address a limb of the law as your poor pet on such
a short acquaintance. I must confess that Tunbridge has
been a difficulty. I have had exhaustive inquiries made.
The Wildes, so far as I can trace them, know no one at

Tunbridge, and you tell me they never visit the place. The letter said "destroy parcel in Tunbridge B.". Why B? The great detective is baffled, I do assure you.'

'You'll be the death of me,' Angela assured him. 'Do you know anything about cabinet-making or Victorian *objets d'art*?'

'I don't collect them.'

'Well, I shall for you — tonight.'

'What do you mean?'

'I haven't the smallest intention of telling you,' said Angela.

CHAPTER 13

The Russian Element

There was a short silence, broken by Angela.

'Does Nigel come with me to the Wildes'?' she asked.

'If you don't mind — no. I've a job for him here. We will both get into the car with you. Vassily will see us out, and we two will leave the car once it is out of sight of the house. There is a garage two hundred yards up the street. Will you park the Bentley there and take a taxi to the Wildes'? When you have got your parcel and had your Tunbridge fun, whatever it is — I'm trusting you there, young woman — please return to — where shall we say? — the Hungaria. I'll book a table. Wait for us there. Do you mind?'

'Of course not,' Angela assured him. 'What are you going to do?'

'Honestly there isn't time to tell you, and you must allow me my smack of officialdom.'

Alleyn rang and Vassily appeared. The inspector told him that he was going back to Frantock and would be away for two days. They put on their coats and hats and three minutes later were looking back at the silhouette of the old butler bowing in the lighted doorway.

Angela drove the car up the cul-de-sac and into Coventry Street, stopping outside the garage Alleyn had indicated. He and Nigel got out.

'*Au revoir,*' said Alleyn, leaning in at the driving-window. 'If we are not at the Hungaria by twelve, ring up this number and ask for Inspector Boys. Quote the code number written on the card, say who you are and ask him to raid my flat.'

'Really?'

'Really. Good hunting.'

'Goodbye darling,' shouted Nigel brazenly, and he and Alleyn walked back towards the flat. Alleyn spoke rapidly.

'Listen carefully, Bathgate. Take a taxi to 128 Little Pryde Street and ask there for Mr Sumiloff. He is working with me on the Russian side of this case and expects a call. Tell him I asked you to communicate with him and that he is to ring up my house and speak to Vassily in Russian. He is to say headquarters are unsafe, but Kuprin suggests an immediate meeting of the committee in my house. If Vassily hesitates, he is to say that I have been watched and have left in the Bentley for Frantock. He is to instruct Vassily and then summon the committee by telephone at once. He is to stress the fact that my house is the most unlikely and therefore the safest rendezvous. He is to suggest a password, and all who arrive at the flat are to use it before gaining admittance. All this Sumiloff is to tell Vassily to organize. I will go over it again. Have you a pencil and paper? Good. Shorthand? Aren't you the clever one? Then note the name, Sumiloff.' Alleyn went over his instructions again.

'I've got that,' said Nigel.

'Sumiloff is then to go to the flat and gain admittance

by the use of the password. He is to say that Kuprin has been arrested for the murder of the Pole, Krasinski, and has asked him to go to the meeting in his stead. He must pitch a yarn to cover himself. Tell him to make certain of Yansen attending the meeting. Yansen cannot speak Russian, only Swedish and English. It is important he should be there. Note that down. That's right. Now off you go.'

'One moment, Alleyn,' said Nigel. 'I understand that Vassily *is* in the thick of it after all.'

'He's in direct and constant communication with the brotherhood, but I do not wish him to think I suspect this. I am under the impression he yearns to be out of it, but dare not say so. I thought it better not to give you these instructions in the flat. Your manner is so very eloquent, Bathgate.'

'Where do I go when the party is on?'

'You? To the Hungaria, where you may inform Miss Angela of the situation. First of all, though, you wait with Sumiloff while he rings up Vassily. If Vassily agrees to receive the committee, you then ring him up yourself— no, wait a bit, that won't do—yes it will. Say you want the Frantock number, as I have asked you to ring me up there tonight. Then go and book a table for three at the Hungaria and wait for us. Goodbye—you'll like Sumiloff —he's a charming fellow. Here's a taxi for you.'

Alleyn held up his stick and a taxi drew up at the kerb. 'We meet,' he said airily, 'at Philippi.'

'128 Little Pryde Street,' said Nigel to the driver.

When he had opened the door and got in, Alleyn had already disappeared.

'Damn it all,' said Nigel to himself, 'I don't in the least know what *he's* going to do.'

Mr Sumiloff was at home and received Nigel. He was a fairish, slightish Russian who spoke excellent English.

'I am delighted to see you,' he told Nigel. 'Alleyn asked

me to hold myself in readiness for a job tonight and mentioned your name. This horrible murder must have been a great shock to you as well as a personal loss. Now please what are our instructions? Let me give you a drink.'

Nigel produced his notes and carefully repeated his lesson.

'I see. A meeting of the committee at Alleyn's flat. What an amusing idea! And Vassily is to receive them and I am to summon them—Yansen, the three Russians, but not Kuprin, who is under arrest. I am to be Kuprin's friend representing him. A little difficult that, but I think I know a way to manage it. Actually, is Kuprin under arrest?'

'I've no idea. Who is Kuprin?'

'He is the leader, the head of the organization in London. He killed Krasinski, no doubt of that. The Yard has been watching the brotherhood for two years, I also, for my friend Alleyn, have been watching and have wormed my way into their council.'

Nigel told him of Tokareff's arrest.

'Do you think Tokareff killed my cousin, Mr Sumiloff?'

'I think—I think it very possible,' said Sumiloff pulling the telephone towards him. He dialled a number and waited.

'Now for Vassily Ivanovitch,' he murmured, and then, 'Hullo, is that Mr Alleyn's flat? Is it Mr Alleyn's servant speaking? Ah—' Then followed a gusty and splashy speech in Russian, long pauses during which the tiny ghost of Vassily's voice spoke from the ear-piece. Finally Sumiloff rang off.

'It's all right so far,' he said. 'Vassily is nervous but obedient. He is evidently terrified of the committee. He says Yansen knows where they all are hiding tonight. The rooms in Soho are watched by the police. He suggests that I ring Yansen up and tell him to collect the others. We may learn a great deal from this meeting. If Tokareff did it, they will certainly discuss his position. Yes—Alleyn has set an amusing trap for them.'

He turned to a memorandum of exchange numbers on his desk and lifted the receiver again. This time the conversation was in English:

'Ah, that you, Number Four? I am the friend of the boss. You remember we have met at his lodgings and at the general council. You know, of course, the boss is taken and also the doctor. I was with the boss when they came for him. He whispered me to call an immediate meeting at—'

Sumiloff broke off to listen to a clatter of expostulation and alarm. A lengthy conversation followed. The bilingual Yansen seemed to be greatly perturbed.

'Those are the boss's instructions,' said Sumiloff, 'The Yard man is safely out of London. Vassily knows and I myself have ascertained this. You know me—Sumiloff. If you like I will come and give my account. It is better not by telephone. Very well. In half an hour at Vassily's, then.' He rang off.

'All right?' asked Nigel.

'I think so.' Sumiloff looked at his watch. 'Nine-thirty.'

'Alleyn said I was to ring Vassily and pretend I wanted the Frantock number. That will confirm Vassily's opinion that Alleyn is out of London.'

'Of course. Will you ring up now, then?'

Nigel dialled the number and in a minute heard Vassily's voice, querulous and elderly. 'Are you there?'

'Hullo, Vassily, is that you?' began Nigel. 'Look here, tell me the Frantock telephone number, will you? I want to get hold of Mr Alleyn as soon as he arrives. It's Mr Bathgate speaking.'

'Jyes, jyes, Mr Bathgate, certainly. It is Frantock 59, sir. The exchange closes at twelve.'

'Thank you so much, Vassily—sorry to bother you.

Good night.'

'So far all right,' said Sumiloff.

Nigel got up.

'Don't go yet. I shan't start myself for twenty minutes. We can leave together,' suggested the Russian. 'Is this your first acquaintance with Inspector Alleyn?'

'Yes. He's an extraordinarily interesting man,' said Nigel. 'Not at all one's idea of a Scotland Yard official.'

'No? Well, I suppose not. He has had an expensive education,' said Sumiloff quaintly. 'He began in the Diplomatic Service; it was then I first met him. It was for private reasons that he became a policeman. It's a remarkable story. Perhaps some day he will tell you.'

As it was evident that Sumiloff himself did not intend further to explain Detective-Inspector Alleyn, Nigel asked him to describe more fully the society whose activities they were investigating. He learnt that the London branch of the brotherhood had been in operation for some years. The organization itself was of amazing antiquity and was strong in the reign of Peter the Great, when it practised various indecent and horrible rites, based on a kind of inverted monasticism.

'One of their favourite practices was to gather together in one house, work themselves into a sort of disgusting frenzy and then lock themselves in and set fire to the building. Unfortunately they did not all do this, so the brotherhood survived to turn itself into a political organization and to associate itself with the doctrines of the Soviet. Whether it has any official recognition I have not been able to discover, though, at Alleyn's suggestion, I have become a member and have gone some way with the ritual.' He glanced at Nigel with a look of curious detachment. 'I am, you see,' he ended, 'a sort of stool pigeon. Unpaid. But I was a patriot once and I do not love the Soviet.'

'And the knife?'

'It is undoubtedly very old. Mongolian, I should say. Its association with the brotherhood is of long standing and it was used for mutilations in the old ritual. It has a hideous history, but the more frantic among the brethren believe that it possesses extraordinary powers. Krasinski had been entrusted to bring it to England after a special meeting of the Society at Geneva—yes, at Geneva, my friend. We shall never know .why he gave it to Mr Rankin. Perhaps he was hard pressed, or frightened, or perhaps he merely wished to leave it with a reliable personage. He was mad. The Poles are even madder than the Russians, Mr Bathgate—and now I must go to my meeting.'

'Where do you imagine Alleyn is at the moment?' asked Nigel as they went downstairs.

Sumiloff did not answer at once. He switched the lights off in his little hall.

'At the moment?' His voice spoke quietly in the dark. 'In his natural habitat, I should think.'

Outside on the footpath a man paused to light his pipe. The match went out and he threw away the box with an exclamation of annoyance.

'Want a light?' asked Sumiloff.

'Thank you very much,' said the man and held out his hand.

'Yard?' asked Sumiloff very quietly.

'Yes, sir. Detailed by Detective-Inspector Alleyn.'

'This gentleman is all right. I am going to the house now. I don't expect trouble, but you know the arrangements, I suppose?'

'Well, sir. Mr Alleyn was very anxious we should keep out of sight, but as soon as the last of them's in the house, we shall close in a bit.'

'I hope you'll be careful. They will certainly set a watch.'

'Yes, sir. We were instructed this afternoon. I understand we don't really mix in at all unless we get a message from the Hungaria restaurant. We are to wait in the empty shop opposite Mr Alleyn's house. The entrance is from the other street, and the young lady is to ring us there. It's an unusual arrangement. Got a whistle, sir?'

'Yes, thank you.' A solitary pedestrian approached.

'Much obliged,' said the Yard man aloud.

'Not at all. Good night.'

Sumiloff and Nigel walked on in silence until they had arrived at Lower Regent Street.

'A whistle might be rather a clumsy method of alarm,' said Nigel, who was eaten up with curiosity.

'Not this one,' rejoined Sumiloff. He produced a little metal disc which he placed under his tongue. 'It is only to be used in an emergency,' he said. 'Perhaps we had better part here.'

'All right. Oh! Half a second. Did you give them a password?'

'Certainly.'

'I say, *do* tell me what it is!'

'You are not grown up yet, I see. Well, there can be no harm. It is the name of the murdered Pole.'

'Great hopping fleas, how dramatic! Good night.'

'Good night, Mr Bathgate.'

Nigel turned into the Hungaria and ordered a table. As he was not in evening dress it was among those at the back of the restaurant. Angela had not yet arrived. Nigel sat down in a state of mental fidget. There were not many people there at this hour and he found little to distract his over-stimulated nerves. He smoked three cigarettes on end, watched three couples dancing an enervated tango, and thought immediately of Rankin and Mrs Wilde.

Another solitary man came in and, after a moment's hesitation, sat down at the next table and ordered lager. The dance band was playing in the desultory manner that distinguishes the off hours in fashionable restaurants.

'Do you want to order, sir?' murmured Nigel's waiter.

'No thank you. I'll wait until my—I'm waiting for someone—I'll order when she comes.'

'Very good, sir.'

Nigel lit a cigarette and tried to picture the scene in Alleyn's house. He wished very much that Angela would come. He wished he were with Sumiloff. He wished he were a detective.

'Excuse me,' said the man at the next table, 'but can you tell me when the Hungarian band comes on?'

'Not until midnight.'

'That's a long time,' said the stranger fretfully. 'I've come on purpose to hear it. Very good, I'm told.'

'Oh, frightfully,' said Nigel unenthusiastically.

'They tell me,' continued his neighbour, 'that some Russian is to sing here tonight. Lovely voice. He sings a thing called *The Death of Boris*.'

Nigel gave a little hop, controlled himself and grunted darkly.

'Everything OK so far?' murmured the man.

This was too exciting! Nigel, with a still greater effort, muttered in the correct Sumiloff manner:

'Yard?'

'Yes. On my way to the appointment. Inspector Boys. Just thought I'd like to hear the latest.'

'Sumiloff has done it,' said Nigel, bending down to fasten his shoe; 'he should be there now.'

'Good enough! Waiter! Can I have my bill?'

A few minutes later he went away, passing Angela, who, with an ill-concealed air of triumph, had appeared in the entrance. She waved to Nigel, wound her way through the tables and sank into the chair the waiter drew out for her.

'Eureka!' said Angela, slapping her handbag down on the table and patting it triumphantly.

'What have you got in there?' asked Nigel quietly.

'I've been to Tunbridge B.'

'Angela, what do you mean? Even you couldn't drive to Tunbridge and back in two hours.'

'Order me some of that delicious-looking lager those people are drinking and I'll reveal everything,' said Angela.

'Beer?' said Nigel in surprise.

'Why not? I adore it. Oceans and oceans of beer,' said Angela extravagantly. 'And now let me tell you what happened. Oh, Nigel,' she continued with a complete change of tone, 'I do *hate* being a spy. If it wasn't for Rosamund I'd never, never have meddled. But I *know* Rosamund didn't do it and—and she's had such a hard row to hoe. Were you fond of Charles, Nigel?'

'I don't know,' said Nigel soberly. 'I've had an awful shock. I've kept on saying to myself "Poor old Charles", but do you know, the only thing I can be certain of is that I didn't really know him. I only accepted him. He was my cousin and all my life I have seen a lot of him. But I didn't know him at all.'

'Rosamund did. She loved him, and it was a terribly unhappy love. Charles behaved very badly. Rosamund has got a ghastly temper, you know. When she was at Newnham she got into no end of a row for—for attacking another undergraduate. There was a terrific scandal. It had started by a lot of them ragging Rosamund about Charles and some other girl, and she flew into a white-hot rage and picked up a knife—yes, a knife—they actually had to hold her back.'

'Good lord!'

'Do you realize that in the dossier Mr Alleyn is making about us all he will have included every shred of our past histories that can have any bearing at all on this case? Be sure there have been exhaustive inquiries into Rosamund's record at Newnham. I *know* she didn't kill Charles, and if it means stealing Marjorie Wilde's letters to prove it—well, anyway I've got them.'

'Letters? You go so fast I can't possibly follow you. Have you stolen some letters?'

'Yes. I guessed, and I'm sure Mr Alleyn did too, that the parcel Marjorie wanted Sandilands to destroy was a bundle of letters. The "Tunbridge B." did puzzle me for a second, but I soon dropped to it. Arthur is very fond of collecting old boxes, and I suddenly remembered him giving Marjorie a funny Victorian casket made out of inlaid wood. Do you know what antique dealers call those caskets?'

'Indeed I don't.'

'Tunbridge boxes. I thought of it at once and in the taxi made up my mind what I should say. Masters, their butler, let me in, and I told him that I had come up to London unexpectedly and was dining out and would he mind if I tidied up in Marjorie's room. The other servants were all out and I was quite undisturbed there. It took me ten minutes to find the box—it was at the back of the top shelf in her wardrobe. Nigel, I—I *picked* the lock with a nail file. It was quite easy, I didn't even break it. I felt like dirt, but I've got the letters. I left my leather coat there, and Masters said if I came back quite late he would still be up, as Mrs Masters was returning from Uxbridge by the last bus. So I'll let Mr Alleyn see them and I hope he will say, "Put them back". Oh, lord, I do feel a swine!'

'I don't think you need, my dear.'

'You're being nice because you like me. Oh, I found out about Sandilands. She was to stay in Dulwich with an ancient aunt, but the aunt's dead, suddenly, and Sandilands has gone to Ealing in a pique. Masters said would I tell Madam because he believed as how there was an arrangement for Madam to write to Sandilands at Dulwich about some garments she was making for Madam. So that fixed that. It was quite easy, and Masters was so agonized with suppressed curiosity about "the unfortunate 'appenings", as he called them, that I really believe he would have let me pocket family portraits without uttering. I don't know why the letters should save Rosamund and I don't know if they are going to involve Marjorie in a scandal, but I've done it.'

'Personally I don't believe the Wildes or Rosamund Grant have anything to do with the murder. I think Tokareff is the man.'

'What about Mary, the pretty tweeny?'

'Well, she *was* the last to see him alive and she *is* pretty and Charles—well, anyway, it was an idea. But still I'm really all for the Russian element. Listen.'

Nigel related his adventures, and Angela was satisfactorily impressed.

'And I actually passed,' she ejaculated, 'a plain-clothes man as I came in. And the police are behind closed shutters in a deserted shop fitted with a telephone, and I am to ring them up if Alleyn doesn't arrive at midnight. How involved!'

'They are afraid to set a more exact watch on Alleyn's house as the Russians are sure to be on the look-out and might suspect something. If Alleyn is there he will probably slip away by a window or—I don't know. Anyway them's orders.'

'What's the time now?'

'Quarter to eleven.'

'Heavens! And we can't even dance. Why didn't Mr Alleyn give us notice of this trip? I could have pleased your eye with my best wisp of tulle. What shall we talk about, Nigel?'

'I should like to talk about love at first sight.'

'Nigel! How entrancing! Have you views on it, or do you rather feel that with such a long wait the only thing is a mild flirtation?'

'No. I have views. But if you are going to make them sound idiotic, I'll keep them to myself.'

'I'm sorry,' said Angela, in a small voice. 'What shall I do?'

'Give me your hand to kiss. They will only think I'm a foreign agent, and I'm so longing to do it.'

Her hand felt cool and rather hard, but his lips persuaded it to be gentle.

'I've got palpitations,' said Nigel suddenly, 'it's very uncomfortable.'

An imperceptible pink mist seemed to have gathered round the table. Angela and Nigel and the beer and the table floated about in the pink mist for half an hour while the band bounced them gently up and down on a delicious tune.

'Excuse me please, sir, but are you Mr Bathgate?' said a waiter suddenly.

'Yes—why?' said Nigel, blinking at him.

'There is a telephone message, sir.'

A piece of paper on a salver appeared under Nigel's nose. He took it and read. The pink mist dissolved, and Nigel sat staring at a dozen words. 'Mr Alleyn hopes Mr Bathgate will join Mr Sumiloff early as possible.'

'Er—thank you, no answer,' said Nigel confusedly.

CHAPTER 14

Meeting Adjourned

Sumiloff's arms were beginning to ache and his legs were agonized with pins and needles. With somewhat unnecessary precaution, they had strapped his wrists and ankles to the chair. The three other Russians were sitting over the empty grate talking intermittently and scarcely glancing at him. Yansen, the Scandinavian, was less detached. He leant across the table where only a little while before Nigel and Angela had tasted Alleyn's port. Yansen was staring at Sumiloff, and had just finished telling him all over again exactly what they proposed to do.

Vassily came into the room. His face was masked with a curious thick pallor. His look at Sumiloff suggested some sort of repressed compassion. He spoke swiftly in Russian and then, for Yansen's benefit, in English.

'The man outside says Mr Bathgate is coming now,' he said.

'We shall receive him,' said Yansen. He turned to the others. 'Are you ready there?' he said. 'It is quite simple. Vassily had better not open the door; if he were to do so it would make an awkwardness.' The others nodded and rose to their feet.

Nigel was in fact turning into the cul-de-sac at that moment. He could not imagine what had necessitated this unexpected move of Alleyn's. Was he to walk into the meeting as if by accident? Was he merely to ask Vassily if a Mr Sumiloff was there or should he give Vassily the password and pretend, unconvincingly, that he was a member of this musical comedy society?

He looked fixedly at the shop opposite Alleyn's house. Was the eye of the Yard observing him from behind those blind shutters? Would he find Alleyn already in possession?

He rang the bell and waited. The man who opened the door obviously was not Vassily. He was younger and taller, but the glare of light behind him prevented Nigel from seeing his face.

'Krasinski,' said Nigel self-consciously.

'That's all right, Mr Bathgate,' replied the man cheerfully. 'Come right in.'

'Well, really!' said Nigel as he walked in. The man shut the door carefully and turned to the light.

'You!' exclaimed Nigel.

'Yes, Mr Bathgate. I was glad to find you at the Hungaria. You told me just what I wanted to know. Will you come along in, sir?'

Nigel followed him to the dining-room. At the door the man stood aside and Nigel, still very bewildered, went in.

Sumiloff was sitting in the wooden chair with his wrists and ankles tied up. Three other men stood up at the far end of the table, and Vassily was behind them.

The man who had been at the Hungaria locked the door and joined the others.

'Sumiloff,' said Nigel, 'what does all this mean?'

'You see for yourself,' said Sumiloff.

'Mr Sumiloff has been a bit indiscreet,' remarked the tall man, 'and so, if you'll excuse me, have you, sir.'

'But,' stammered Nigel, 'is Sumiloff one of the society, then?'

'On the contrary, I am. Not Detective-Inspector Boys, Mr Bathgate, but Erik Yansen. Allow me to present my comrades. We are all armed and you are covered, Mr Bathgate.'

While they were binding him to the other armchair, Nigel's predominant thought was what a fool Angela would think him. And what a triple-damnable fool Alleyn would think him, he reflected, as the leather strap bit into his ankle. He looked at Sumiloff.

'How has it happened?' he asked.

'Yansen saw us together in Regent Street. It is my fault. It was criminally careless; we should never have gone so far together. He recognized me and, being already suspicious, followed you to the Hungaria.'

'Quite correct,' said Yansen. 'And since our Comrade Vassily had told us how puzzled Mr Alleyn is with the doctor's song, I ventured to mention it. Your face encouraged me to proceed, Mr Bathgate.'

'Detective-Inspector Alleyn,' said Nigel, 'has told me my face is eloquent.'

'So when I arrived here, we arranged to send you a little message.'

'It's all beautifully clear now, thank you,' said Nigel.

'Before the arrival of Comrade Yansen, however,' said Sumiloff suddenly, 'I was able to collect an appreciable amount of information. Tokareff did not murder your cousin, Mr Bathgate.'

Vassily exclaimed abruptly in Russian, and was answered peremptorily by one of his compatriots.

'It would have been big glory for him if he had killed zis man,' added the Russian heavily.

'Nonsense,' said Sumiloff loudly.

The Russian who had spoken walked across the room and hit Sumiloff across the mouth.

'*Svinya!*' said Sumiloff disinterestedly. 'He is upset because I do not know where Alleyn is. Look at the room.'

It had begun to dawn on Nigel that the house was in a chaotic state of disruption. The curtains had been dragged aside, the furniture pulled out from the walls, a desk had been opened, and the great open fireplace was littered with papers. He remembered noticing the same sort of disorder in the hall.

'They have been down into the cellars and up into the attic too,' said Sumiloff. 'Now they do not know what to do with us.'

'Listen to me,' said Yansen forcibly. 'One of you or both of you can tell us what Alleyn is doing. Give us some line on where he is. It is ridiculous to refuse, to oblige us to use force.'

He stood over Nigel.

'Where is Alleyn?' he said.

'I have no idea,' said Nigel. 'It is the truth—I do not know.'

'When and where did you arrange to meet him after—this?'

'I made no arrangements.'

'Lying pig,' whispered Yansen vehemently. He slapped Nigel's face, knocking the back of his head against the chair. The Russians began talking together.

'What are you saying?' demanded Yansen.

'Shall I interpret?' offered Sumiloff sweetly.

'*Niet!* No!' said the tallest of the three. 'I can myself make it all right in English. I say give them some torments to talk. There is no time for waiting. It is not safe. Then afterwards what to do with them? I think better to kill them bose, but then for dispose the bodies? It is difficult. But first make them spik.'

The clock in the little hall cleared its throat and struck twelve. Angela would ring up now, the police were just across the street. There was no need to get the wind up. Vassily suddenly burst out crying: the embarrassing tears of an old man. The Russians apparently cursed him, and the one who could speak English came over to Sumiloff, fingering the lapel of his coat. They spoke together in Russian.

'Bathgate,' said Sumiloff quietly, 'they are going to run a pin up my nails. And yours too. It is rather an infantile form of torture, and not at all up to the traditions of the brotherhood. But it hurts.'

He ended with a quick intake of his breath. Nigel heard himself cursing. Yansen and one of the Russians bent over him. Nigel remembered a remark of Arthur Wilde's: 'It should be possible so to divorce the mind from the body that one could look on at one's own physical pain with the same analytical detachment one directs towards the agony of another person.'

A sickening and disgusting pain violated his fingers. His whole body jerked and the straps cut his flesh. 'I shall not be able to bear this,' he thought. Vassily was sobbing loudly. The four men stood over Sumiloff and Nigel. Nigel shut his eyes.

'Now,' said Yansen, 'you will tell us—where is Alleyn?'

'Immediately behind you,' said Alleyn.

A sort of blare of amazement lit up inside Nigel's brain. Close to his ear someone was blowing an ear-splitting whistle. The noise corresponded precisely with the pain in his fingertips. He opened his eyes. A nigger minstrel with a revolver squatted, straddle-legged over the dead fire.

'No funny business,' said this apparition. 'You're covered all round, you know. Put 'em up, my poppets.'

The room was full of men—policemen and men in dark suits. Nigel was unbound, but he still sat in his arm-chair staring at the black-faced Alleyn who talked busily to Sumiloff.

'I knew it was possible to get up that chimney,' he said, 'they had a photo of it in *The Ideal Home*, and they said, "Lovely old-world chimney, untouched since the days when the master-sweep sent his boy up to the roof". "Untouched" is the word, witness my face. I'm no boy, and it was a damn' tight squeeze, and hellish hot too. Got your men, Boys? Right you are—take 'em off.'

'How about the old chap?' asked a burly gentleman whom Nigel rightly took to be the true Inspector Boys.

'Vassily? No. He's an old fool, but he's not under arrest. I'll be along to the station when I've cleaned up.'

'Roighto, sir,' said Inspector Boys richly. 'Come along, please, gentlemen.' In a few minutes the front door slammed.

'Vassily,' said Alleyn, 'no more brotherhoods for you. Get some iodine, tidy up, produce drinks, run a hot bath, and get the Hungaria on the telephone.'

Nigel could scarcely believe only an hour had elapsed since he had left Angela. She was looking very worried and seemed immensely pleased and relieved at his arrival. She fussed over his finger, appeared horror-stricken at his narrative, and made him feel a hero instead of the fool he knew he had been. They ate some bacon, Nigel paid the bill and, being much in love with Angela, thought the drive back to Frantock all too short.

Bunce, PC, held them up at the gates and they fed him with a few morsels of news. Frantock was in darkness and the hall with its dying fire eerily reminiscent of Sunday's tragedy. Nigel kissed Angela gently as she stood with her lighted candle at the head of the stairs.

'With Tokareff off the list,' she said suddenly, 'it narrows matters down a bit. Nigel, do you think Mr Alleyn means it when he says he no longer suspects— us?'

'Goodness, darling, what a thought to go to bed with! Why, of course—anything else is unthinkable. Would he trust us as he has done, otherwise?'

'It seems to me,' said Angela, 'that he trusts nobody. What am I to do with these letters?'

'Give them to me. I'll show them to him tomorrow, and perhaps we can go up to London after the inquest and return them "unbeknownst".'

'Yes, perhaps,' said Angela. 'Thank you very much, Nigel dear, but if you don't mind I'll keep them till then myself.' She kissed him suddenly, whispered 'Good night' and went away.

Nigel undressed and slipped into bed. The throbbing pain in his finger kept him awake for a little while, but at last, amidst a crowd of grotesque faces mouthing in the semblance of Sumiloff, Vassily, Yansen, and the three Comrades, he fell backwards into a fast car and with a nervous leap of his pulses drove down through whirling night into nothingness.

The inquest was held in Little Frantock at eleven o'clock the next morning. It took a very much shorter time and was altogether less formidable than any of the house-party had anticipated. Nigel had, of course, already been informed of the nature of Rankin's will. Charles had left the bulk of his property to Nigel himself, together with his house and furniture, but there were several legacies, including a sum of three thousand pounds to Arthur Wilde and a bequest of books, pictures, and *objets d'art* to Sir Hubert Handesley. The terms of the

will were brought up at the inquest, and Nigel felt that he
looked exactly like a murderer, but otherwise came
remarkably little into the picture. The coroner spent some
time over Mary the 'tweenmaid's evidence, and put a
good many questions to Arthur Wilde, these two having
been the last to speak to Rankin. A great deal of time was
spent over the Russian element. Alleyn gave a brief,
colourless account of the meeting of the Comrades and
emphasized the point that he had clearly overheard them
all state definitely that Tokareff had had no hand in the
murder. Sumiloff was called and supported Alleyn on this
point. A remarkably plain and dowdy little lawyer
'watched' the proceedings on behalf of Doctor Tokareff.
The treasonable and theatrical goings-on of the brotherhood caused a considerable sensation.

Rosamund Grant was not called, but Mrs Wilde,
wearing rouge on her mouth but none on her face,
supported Wilde in their own account of their joint
conversation during the time of the murder. Sir Hubert,
seeming terribly shaken, was treated with elaborate
courtesy by the coroner. The incident of the willing of the
knife by Rankin to Sir Hubert was touched on, but the
coroner made little of it.

Alleyn asked for an adjournment; the whole affair
ended, leaving the onlookers with a sense of having been
served with treason when they ordered murder.

The guests were now at liberty to leave Frantock, and
Nigel's house-party was at an end. He was faced with the
prospect of returning to his newspaper office, replete with
forbidden copy. The office had been heavily tactful.
Jamison, his chief, had rung him up, telling him rather
wistfully not to worry. Nigel pictured the news-hungry
Scot and, grinning to himself, had actually spent an hour
before the inquest writing up the Russian element.

Now he stood for the last time at his window in the little
Welsh room, listening to the querulous overtones of Mrs

Wilde's voice as she talked to her husband amid their suit-cases, beyond the bathroom. Angela had disappeared immediately after the inquest, presumably with the object of hurrying up to London with the letters. Nigel had had no opportunity of talking to her, and felt rather injured. With a sigh he turned from the window and laid a pound note on the dressing-table for Ethel the Intelligent. A whole pound! Handsome and rather extravagant, but, after all, she had seen him before the lights went out and thus, he reflected, established his alibi.

There was a tap on the door.

'Come in,' said Nigel.

It was Sir Hubert. He came in uncertainly, hesitated at sound of the Wildes' voices and then, turning away from Nigel, spoke softly.

'I only interrupted you,' he said, 'to tell you, while there is an opportunity, how deeply I feel—' he hesitated and then went on more vigorously—'how deeply I regret the tragic circumstances of your first visit here, Bathgate.'

'Oh, please, sir—' began Nigel, but the other inter-rupted him.

'You are going to be polite and generous about it, I know; but, though that is very nice of you, it does not make very much difference to what has happened. I feel —horribly responsible to you all, but particularly to you. If I can ever be of any use to you, you must promise to let me know.'

'It is very kind of you,' answered Nigel impulsively. 'I do hope you will try, sir, if it's not an impertinence for me to talk like this, to get rid of any feeling of morbid responsibility to any of us. I—I was fond of Charles, naturally, but I do not believe I knew him half as well as you. I think that you—his greatest friend, after all—feel his death most of any of us.'

'I was extremely fond of him,' said Handesley, tone-lessly.

'You know, of course, that he has left you a number of pictures and things. I shall see that they are sent here as soon as everything is settled up. If there is anything else among his possessions that you know of and would like to have as—a remembrance of Charles, I do hope you will let me know. This sounds awful, but I thought—' Nigel paused uncomfortably.

'Thank you very much indeed. I do perfectly understand, but I am sure there is nothing—' Handesley turned towards the window, 'except perhaps the dagger. As you know, that will be mine in any case. I believe the will is quite in order.'

For two or three seconds Nigel was literally unable to speak. He stared at the back of Sir Hubert's distinguished white head and thoughts of the complete incalculability of human reactions raced in utter confusion through his mind.

'Of course—' he heard himself say. Handesley interrupted him.

'You think it very strange that I should want to possess this weapon,' he said. 'To you, perhaps, it is strange, but you are not a passionately enthusiastic collector, nor have you the detached point of view of the student. This knife cannot remind me more forcibly of that which, in any case, I can never forget, but it seems to me that it is due to Charles's memory that I should have it when once the police have finished with it. You do not understand this, but Charles himself, who knew my character, would have understood. I think anyone interested in such things as I am interested would also understand. It is the scientific point of view.'

'What's this about the scientific point of view?' asked Wilde, poking his head round the bathroom door. 'Sorry if I'm interrupting, but I heard the phrase.'

'You should be able to interpret it, Arthur,' rejoined Sir Hubert. 'I must go down and relieve Rosamund. She is terribly upset still and Alleyn insisted on interviewing her again today. Arthur, tell me, do you think—?'

'I've given up thinking,' said Arthur Wilde bitterly.

Nigel saw Handesley as he went out steal a glance at his old friend.

'What's the matter with Hubert?' asked Wilde when they were alone.

'Don't ask me,' said Nigel wearily. 'This crime seems to have acted like a corrosive acid in all our hearts. Do you know, he wants to have the dagger?'

'What!'

'Yes. He reminded me of that will you witnessed—you remember, the joke will.'

'I remember,' said Wilde, sitting on the bed and staring blankly at Nigel through his glasses.

'He said you would understand.'

'The scientific point of view. I see. How terribly consistent! Yes, I suppose in a way I do understand, but— good lord!'

'I know. Have a cigarette.'

'Arthur!' called Mrs Wilde from beyond the bathroom. 'Have you rung up and told them what time we are arriving tonight? I do wish you wouldn't wander off like that.'

'Coming, darling,' said Wilde. He hurried back to his wife, and Nigel, wondering if Angela had returned, went out on to the landing. He met Alleyn at the head of the stairs.

'I was looking for you,' said the chief inspector. 'Can you come down to the study for a moment?'

'With pleasure,' answered Nigel drearily. 'What's up now? Are you going to tell me you've discovered the murderer?'

'Well, as a matter of fact, I am,' said Alleyn.

CHAPTER 15

Alleyn Comes Cleanish

'Did you mean that?' asked Nigel as the detective closed the door behind them.

'Yes, it's true. I know now. I have known for some time, I think; but even though a Yard official is supposed to have no psyche, I find there is often a moment in a case when a piece of one's mind, one's feeling, one's sense, knows the end while all the rest of the trained brain cuts this intuitive bit dead. Yes, it's like that sometimes.'

'Who is it?'

'It is not for the sake of keeping you on tenterhooks that I don't answer that at once. I want someone to listen to the evidence. Oh, we've gone over it at the Yard *ad infinitum*, of course. There are one or two of us who know the case-book off by heart. But I want to hear myself repeating it to someone fresh. Will you be patient, Bathgate?'

'Very well, only, God knows, it's not easy.'

'I'll be as brief, and as impersonal, as possible. The policeman speaking. On Monday morning when I began work on this case I interviewed the members of this house-party individually and afterwards, as you remember, together. At the conclusion of our "trial" I made an exhaustive examination of the house. With the assistance of Bunce, I reconstructed the murder. The position of the body (which had been so infuriatingly interfered with), of the knife, of the cocktail shaker and of the gong, led me to assume that Rankin had been stabbed from behind and from above. It is no easy matter to drive a knife into a body from the back so as to penetrate the heart. This had been accomplished, and I, with Doctor Young, suspected a certain anatomical knowledge. Who of the party possessed such knowledge? Doctor Tokareff. For some time the evidence pointed strongly towards Doctor Tokareff, and the fantastic aspect of the motive was considerably upheld by the murder of Krasinski for the same reason—the violation of the sacred dagger. Two objections withheld me from going definitely for the Russian—one, the fact that he is left-handed, the other the distance from his room to the scene of the murder. Also I gathered that he strongly urged the inadvisability of moving the body.

'His attitude, too, was hard to explain. He made no attempt to disguise his indifference to Rankin's death and his feeling that it was an act of poetic justice. Next I turned my attention to Rosamund Grant. Here was had the age-old motive of the woman, not exactly scorned, but faced with complete disillusion as regards the man she passionately loved. She was aware of Rankin's intrigue with Mrs Wilde. She had tried to see him, had lied about her movements immediately prior to the murder, and in my interview with her was an extremely unsatisfactory subject. She had studied anatomy and had in the past given exhibitions of an ungovernable and violent temper. Miss Angela's discovery of a wisp of green fluff from her shoe in Rankin's room was a fortunate event for Miss Grant. It cut down the time factor in her case to an almost impossible ration. Then Sir Hubert. Here the only motive I could discover was the passion of the collector. This passion can become a disease, and I am not sure that Sir Hubert is not tainted with it. He has gone to extraordinary lengths to add to his collection. But murder? And again the time factor. In your case I was extremely thorough, but the housemaid's evidence was unanswerable; you had smoked two cigarettes while you were in your room, too. You were not in debt. Money is the motive behind most crimes, and in your case it was there—nice and healthy. I gave you up with reluctance.

'Well, so it went on. Mrs Wilde, who, from the scene you and Miss Grant overheard, revealed herself to be in a state of hysterical and reluctant subjection to Rankin, was too short to have accomplished the murder. Her husband had revealed an interesting phobia of hers as regards knives and blades of all sorts. She was in debt. Rankin left her husband three thousand. Also she had lugged the body some way out of position—a noteworthy point. But she was too short. This led me back to the position of the assailant, and I put Bunce in Rankin's place and myself stood behind him at the foot of the stairs. If I stood on the bottom step I could not reach him, and I was persuaded the victim had been standing by the cocktail tray. From the floor, even I could scarcely get the correct down-drive indicated by the position of the dagger. Where, then, had the assailant stood? How had he drawn so close without being observed and yet—! Every time I seemed to end up in a cul-de-sac. I had, of course, got all your fingerprints. We went over every inch of the walls and the banisters. The knife-handle gave no prints. Then at last we made another discovery. Amongst the confused blur of prints on the knob at the bottom of the banister were the faint but unmistakable impressions left by two hands that had gripped it from above. The left hand was moderately clear, but the right hand was quite a different proposition. It was the curious impression left by a gloved hand, and the pressure had been great enough to show the actual seams of the glove and in places an indication of the coarse-grained leather. They were bad prints, but we got a good enough impression from them to suggest they had been made by the right and left hands of the same individual. Their angle was curious. It called up the picture of someone standing with their back to the stairs leaning across the curved end of the banister at a very

awkward angle. A most unlikely attitude, unless—'
Alleyn paused.

'Well?' said Nigel.

'Unless the person who made them was sitting astride
the banister and facing the hall. Someone who had, for
instance, slid down the banister and fetched up leaning
heavily on the knob. A person with a longish reach could,
from that position, have just got hold of the knife as it
hung on the leather strip against the wall. Such a person
would have been considerably higher than the stooping
victim. We re-examined the entire length of the rail. At
the top we found similar prints consistent with my idea
that their author had slid down the banister face first. I
asked Miss Angela if any of you had been indulging in
this mild sport and she told me no—not this weekend. I
also ascertained that Doctor Tokareff and Mrs Wilde
were no good at it. This was not particularly interesting as
the prints were not those of any of these persons.'

'Then whose—?'

'We next turned our attention to the outer border of the
bottom of the banister, the wooden base into which the
uprights are set. Here we found a print, solitary and
unmistakable, since Ethel, Mary and Co. don't fancy
poking a duster through the rails. It was incisive at the top
and blurred farther down.'

'But how could anyone get their hand through the rails,
and why should they?'

'It was not the print of a hand, but of a naked foot, a
foot that had just brushed the wood as its owner slid down
the banister. And with that discovery, I had to reconstruct
my ideas about the time factor. It gave me about ten
seconds more room to think about in. A vivid little scene
had begun to take shape. Picture it, Bathgate. The hall is
dimly lit. Mary has turned off most of the lights, having a
mania for this manoeuvre. She has gone out and Rankin
is bending over the cocktail tray, clearly lit by the wall-

lamp above it. The stairs are practically in darkness.
Rankin is probably shaking up the last of the cocktail,
preparatory to pouring it out. At the top of the stairs
appears a dim, half-clad figure. It may be wearing a
dressing-gown or perhaps it is only clad in underclothes.
A glove is on its right hand. There is a faint swishing
noise, drowned by the gurgle of the cocktail shaker. The
figure is now astride the bottom of the banister. It makes
two swift gestures and Rankin pitches forward, striking
the gong with his head. The figure on the banister leans
far out and reaches towards the switch. Then complete
darkness.'

Alleyn stopped speaking.

'Well,' ventured Nigel with shaky facetiousness. 'Am I
now supposed to know the answer?'

Alleyn looked at him with a curious air of compassion.

'Not even yet?' he said.

'Whose were the prints?'

'That I am not going to tell you. Oh, believe me,
Bathgate, not out of any desire to figure as the mysterious
omnipotent detective. That would be impossibly vulgar.
No. I am not telling you because there is still that bit of
my brains that cannot quite accept the QED of the
theorem. There is only one tangible bit of evidence in this
whole case. That is the button of the glove worn by the
murderer. The glove was burnt, but the fastening, a
press-button, was recovered. The miserable little button
fastens the whole structure of my case. It is not enough.
So I have decided to make an extraordinary experiment,
Bathgate. I am going to ask the group of suspected
persons to look on while we go through a performance of
the murder. One of the guests must slide down the
banister and in dumb-show re-enact that terrible little
scene. I want you, with the "very comment of your
soul", if that was the phrase, to observe the others. Yes,
it's Hamlet's old stunt over again, and if it comes off I

hope I shan't make the muck he did of the result. You have made some friends here, haven't you?'

'Yes,' answered Nigel, surprised.

'Then I am afraid the result is going to come as a shock to you. For that reason I have told you this much. I have enjoyed your companionship, Bathgate,' ended the chief inspector with one of those curious twists of formality that Nigel had grown accustomed to. 'Perhaps we may have a final talk together—afterwards.'

'I shall insist on it,' Nigel assured him.

'Well! Do one last job of work for me. Will you play the murderer's part in the play within the play and help me to trick this shadowy figure into betraying itself?'

'I must say—' said Nigel coldly.

'Ah! you don't care to do it. It is detestable to you. I hate illogical sentimentality. It is so conceited.'

There was a note of bitterness in Alleyn's voice that Nigel had not heard before.

'You don't understand—' he began.

'I think I do. For you it's all over. Rankin was your cousin; you have had a shock. You have also, you must confess, enjoyed the part you have played up to date in helping to round up a bunch of mad Russians. But now, when a criminal who is prepared—even schemes—to let an innocent person hang, turns out to be someone you know, you become all fastidiousness and leave the dirt to the policeman. Quite understandable. In a couple of years you will be dining out on this murder. Pity you can't write it up.'

'You're unfair,' said Nigel angrily.

'Am I? Well don't let's quarrel. Perhaps you wouldn't mind asking Bunce, who is out on the drive, to report to me. I am afraid that it is part of my schedule that you should witness, with the others, this final scene. Your train goes in half an hour.'

Nigel walked to the door. 'I'll tell Bunce,' he volunteered.

'Thank you,' said Alleyn wearily.

'And,' continued Nigel rather indistinctly, 'I still think you are unfair, Alleyn, but if you like, if you'll allow me to—I'll do whatever you suggest to help.'

Alleyn's singularly charming smile lightened his eyes for a moment.

'All right,' he said. 'Sorry! I'm a bundle of nerves at the moment, and I do so hate murders. Perhaps someone else will do, after all. Come back with the bluebottle and I'll explain.'

Nigel found Bunce, PC, staring disconsolately at a dead chrysanthemum in a border by the side lawn.

'Detective Chief Inspector Alleyn wants you in the study,' said Nigel, enjoying the rhythmic sequence of the titles and name.

'Oh!' said Bunce, rousing himself. 'Thank you, sir. I'll come along. It'll be a bit of a change after these urbashus borders. I'm not a great Nature-lover myself.'

'No?'

'No. Altogether too 'ap'azard to my way of thinking. Sloppy. That's Nature. Well, I'll be shifting.'

'I'm coming too,' said Nigel, and they returned in silence to the study.

Alleyn was standing by the fireplace examining a revolver. He slipped it into his pocket.

'Bunce,' he said crisply, 'have a man outside the front door in ten minutes' time, another in the drawing-room and a third here. The members of the household will then be assembled in the hall. Keep your wits about you and your ears well open. When you hear me say, "Now, let us begin", come very quietly into the hall and keep the person, of whom I have already informed you, under observation. I expect no trouble, but—well, the quieter the better. The arrest will probably take place immediately. By the way, I shall want you to impersonate the victim as you did during the first reconstruction.'

Bunce's eyes lightened.

'Very good, sir. 'Ead first into the gong as usual, I presoom?'

'Yes, Bunce. You may retain your helmet if you like.'

''Ardly artistic would it be, sir? I shan't notice the blow in my excitement.'

'As you please. Very well, then, off you go. Place your men now, will you? And don't discuss anything. That clear?'

'Abundantly, sir,' ejaculated Bunce. He turned about smartly and left the room by the french window.

'Now, Bathgate,' said Alleyn, 'I shall make certain of everybody being in the hall in half an hour. The cars will be outside to take you all to the station. Miss Angela has just returned so we shall be complete — with the exception of the Russians, of course. By the way, Bathgate, can you slide down banisters face first?'

'I'm not sure. I think so.'

'Well, it may not be necessary — I'll spare you if I can. Would you mind ringing that bell?'

The summons was answered by the ubiquitous Ethel.

'Would you find Miss North, Ethel?' asked the inspector. 'Ask her, if it is not very inconvenient, to speak to me for a moment.'

'Very good, sir.'

Angela came in looking as if the drive up to London had agreed with her.

'I put back the letters quite successfully,' she said, 'but I do wish you hadn't kept those two. It makes me feel abominable. Where are they?'

'At the police station,' Alleyn told her. 'They proved to be of considerable value. You need not feel abominable. All you have done is to save Mrs Wilde from the indignity of an official search through her house. Your part in obtaining the letters will never appear.'

'That's not quite the point,' objected Angela. 'I've

played Marjorie a dirty trick, but if it's helped Rosamund—'

'It has helped to establish evidence which I needed,' said Alleyn firmly. 'I cannot see that anything else is of consequence. I am unable to feel any sympathy with the incalculable megrims of the layman.'

'You are not very human this morning,' said Angela unsteadily.

'So Bathgate has intimated. If you feel qualms in your conscience on Mrs Wilde's account, you shall be given ample opportunities of helping her. Has she any great woman friend?'

'I don't know,' said Angela nervously. 'I don't really believe she has.'

'That sort don't as a rule. ''Cats that walk by their wild lone''.'

'I have never liked you less,' said Angela vigorously.

'I seem to be generally unpopular. However, that, too, is irrelevant. I have only asked to see you for a moment in order to say that I would be deeply grateful if you could muster your guests and Sir Hubert for the last time in the hall. Perhaps you could suggest that there is just time for a cocktail before they leave for the train.'

'Certainly,' said Angela rather grandly.

Alleyn was ahead of Nigel in opening the door to her. He looked at her very searchingly.

'A policeman's lot is not a happy one,' he said wryly. 'This case has now reached a point which I invariably find almost intolerable. Will you remember that?'

Angela had turned rather pale.

'Very well,' she said, 'I'll remember,' and went away on her errand.

'Now, Bathgate,' said Alleyn, go out into the hall and keep quiet and don't look as if anything in particular is afoot. Remember—I want as many unbiased records as possible of the reconstruction. Off with you, for heaven's sake. The buzzer is ringing, the house-lights are down, the curtain's going up. Take your seats, ladies and gentlemen, for the last act.'

CHAPTER 16

The Accused was Charged

The house-party was assembled for the last time in the hall at Frantock. The grouping, the lighting, the clothes, the faces, the background, were all much as they had been on that previous Sunday not yet a week ago. It was a repetition of the same theme in a minor key, a theme less rich, impoverished since it lacked the colour of Rankin's verve and Tokareff's robust vowels.

The cocktail tray was in its accustomed place. No one stood near it. It was as though the ghost of Rankin's body set up a barrier there and were best avoided.

Sir Hubert came slowly down the stairs and joined his guests. He seemed to feel some obligation to smother the dismal silence with words and made painfully disjointed conversation to Wilde and Nigel, who answered him with punctilious constraint. The others were quite silent. The cars would come soon and they just waited.

The study door opened and Alleyn came through into the hall. They all looked at him warily, united in a profound and subtle antagonism. In their thoughts, so secret to each other, they were yet conscious of this one common feeling of enmity to the detective. Perhaps, thought Nigel, it is an instinctive animal opposition to discipline. They waited for the detective to speak. He walked into the centre of the hall and faced them.

'May I ask for your attention?' he began formally. 'I have been obliged to detain you here until the inquest, a delay of four days which I realize many of you have found inconvenient and all of you extremely distasteful. This restriction is now withdrawn, and in a few minutes Frantock will be left to its own meditations. Before you go, however, I have decided to let you all understand the theory of the police as to the manner in which the crime was committed.'

He paused, and a dead, shocked silence held the echo of his voice. After a moment he began to speak again:

'The simplest way of making myself clearly understood is to reconstruct the machinery of the murder. To do this I must ask for your assistance. We shall need two persons to play the parts of the victim and of the murderer as the police have visualized them. Perhaps someone will volunteer to give me this much assistance.'

'No—oh no—no!' Mrs Wilde's voice, shrill and out of tune, disconcerted them by its vehemence.

'Steady, darling,' said Arthur Wilde quietly. 'It's all right. It will be better for all of us to learn everything that Inspector Alleyn can tell us. It is very largely our ignorance of the official theory that has made this suspense intolerable.'

'I agree, Arthur,' said Handesley. He turned to Alleyn. 'If I can be of any help I am quite willing.'

Alleyn looked steadily at him.

'Thank you very much indeed, Sir Hubert, but I think I won't ask you to perform the curious feat that I believe to be necessary. I want a man who can slide down the banister—face foremost.'

'I am afraid I cannot quite do that,' said Handesley after a long pause.

'No. Perhaps you, Mr Wilde?'

'I?' said Wilde. 'Well, I'm getting a bit stiff in the joints for that sort of exercise, Inspector.'

'Still, I understand you have accomplished it before, so if you don't mind—'

'Very well,' agreed Wilde, and Nigel felt that Alleyn was letting him off a piece of pantomime he had been so loath to perform.

'Now,' Alleyn continued. 'I shall get the constable who assisted me before to impersonate Mr Rankin as that, perhaps, would be too painful an obligation to put upon any of his friends. Are you there, Bunce?' he said loudly. The officer emerged from the study.

'Just stand as you did before, will you?' said Alleyn.

The constable moved to the cocktail tray, picked up the shaker and bent over with his back to the stairs.

'Thank you,' said Alleyn, 'that will do. Now, Mr Wilde. It is my theory that the murderer slid down the banister rail, took the knife from the leather strip on the wall there with his right hand, leant across and drove it home. Will you mimic his movements along those lines?'

'It seems a bit fantastic,' said Wilde dubiously.

'Doesn't it? Let us begin.'

Another silence and then Wilde slowly climbed the stairs. Two men had appeared in the hall, standing unobtrusively in the dining-room and drawing-room doorways. A third could be seen darkly through the glass door into the entrance lobby.

The lights, with the exception of the wall bracket above the cocktail tray, had all been switched off.

'What exactly is the procedure?' Wilde's voice sounded plaintively from the shadowy stair-head.

Alleyn repeated his description.

'I'm not a star performer at this,' murmured the voice.

'Never mind—do your best.'

The slight figure could scarcely be seen straddling the banister. It began to move towards them very slowly, its spectacles gleaming a little in the dark.

'I can't stand it!' screamed a woman's voice suddenly. It was Mrs Wilde. Nigel, resting his hands against Rosamund Grant's chair, could feel it shaking.

'Faster!' said Alleyn urgently.

Wilde, leaning back and gripping the rail with his knees, shot downwards into the light.

'Now — now the knife,' cried Alleyn.

'I — don't — quite — understand.'

'Yes you do. With your right hand. Reach out to the leather strip. Lean over — farther. Now — you have seized the knife. Lean over the other way. Watch him, watch carefully. Lean over the over way, man — but quick — quick as lightning. Now — strike down at him. *Do as I tell you!*'

The straddling figure moved its arm. Bunce fell forward. The great voice of the gong sounded again — ominous and intolerable. Through it the detective's voice rose excitedly.

'There — there! That's how it was. Turn all the lights on. Don't move, Mr Wilde. You are fully dressed now, you know. Lights, Bathgate!'

Nigel switched on the central candelabra. The hall was flooded with a hard white light.

Wilde still sat astride the banister. His face, contorted into a horrible grimace, shone clammily. One corner of his mouth twitched. Alleyn moved swiftly towards him.

'Excellent,' he said, 'only you should have been quicker — and you had forgotten something. Look here!' He suddenly thrust a yellow dogskin glove in front of Wilde's face.

'That yours?' he said.

'God rot your bloody soul!' said Arthur Wilde.

'Arrest him,' said Alleyn.

Nigel stared out of his carriage window at a rapidly diminishing group of wintry trees through whose ghostly branches glowed the warmth of old brick. A blue spiral of threadbare smoke rose from one of the chimneys, wavering uncertainly and spreading like a wraith of the treeshapes beneath it. A little figure moved across the home field where Nigel had walked with Handesley. Already it was growing dark and a fragile mist skirted the woods.

'Goodbye, Frantock,' said Alleyn.

The train roared into a cutting and the picture was turned into a dream.

'For you, Bathgate, *au revoir*, I suppose?'

'Who knows?' murmured Nigel, and the detective did not answer.

For a long time neither of them spoke. Alleyn wrote in his little note-book. Nigel thought confusedly of his strange adventures and of Angela. At last, with his eyes on the fast-darkening window-pane, he asked his question: 'When were you first positive of him?'

Alleyn pressed a wisp of tobacco down into the bowl of his pipe.

'I don't know,' he said at last. 'Do you realize that it was you who, from the very beginning, led me up the garden path?'

'I? What do you mean?'

'Can't you see—can't you see? You swore over and over again that during that fatal five minutes you were talking continuously to Arthur Wilde. So did his goat of a wife, poor little devil! She didn't suspect him—she was terrified for herself. Oh, I know you said so in all good faith. You thought he had been talking all the time. Of course you did. You had an unconscious mental picture of Arthur Wilde lying in his tub and washing behind his ears. You heard all the suitable noises—splashy, soapy noises, running taps, and so on. If you could have seen!'

'Seen?'

'Seen through the wall. If only the wall had been like a transparency on the stage. If you could have seen Wilde come into the bathroom, wearing those silly little underpants Rankin had laughed at, as you told me, I remember, that very afternoon! You would have watched him lean over the bath, turn on the taps, splash about with his hands and move his lips as he spoke to you. You would have watched that inglorious little figure wipe his hands carefully, run into his wife's dressing-room and come back with one glove on. He had a nerve-racking hunt for the left-hand glove but he had scuffled it over the back of the drawer in his hurry and it had fallen down through a gap in the old casing. How you would have gaped when he opened the door and (perhaps calling out to you first) peeped on to the landing and then, just as Ethel the housemaid entered your room, slipped out. Eight seconds later the gong sounded and the bathroom was blotted out in darkness so that you would not have seen the figure return, pull off his clothes and tumble into the bath. Still he talked to you while he washed and washed in case any of Rankin's blood had splashed his body. It must have been awful waiting for the lights to show him if the glove was stained. I expect he pushed it into his pocket to wait until later when Mrs Wilde was having hysterics in the drawing-room and you others were all clustered round her. That was his chance, I dare say, to run into the hall and thrust his wife's dogskin glove into the fire and heap coal over it. The press-button would have gone with the rest if it hadn't dropped down between the bars into the tray beneath. That, with the left-hand glove, was my one exhibit. He kept his head pretty well. Even remembered to say "You are the corpse" to someone on the landing. This was bound to come out with the rest of the evidence and it made a very good impression.'

'Why did he do it?' Nigel asked.

'Ah, the motive—or motives rather. Primarily, money. Wilde's wife owes a thousand to various dressmakers. He is dunned by his landlord, and is deeply involved otherwise, and he lost heavily on his last book. He knew Rankin was leaving him three thousand pounds.

Secondarily, we have two very interesting reasons why
Wilde should have cause to welcome, if not to compass,
Rankin's death. He hated your cousin. I have gone
extensively into their past relationship. Rankin bullied
and goaded Wilde when they were at Eton. He showed a
sort of contemptuous disregard for him in their later
relations. I have learned from the waiters at night clubs,
from a dismissed lady's maid, and from you in your
unsuspecting account of the ragging on Sunday, that
Rankin flirted openly with Mrs Wilde under the very nose
of her supposedly good-natured, mild, and absent-
minded husband. He had read Rankin's letters. Here I
had a stroke of luck. The packet of letters Miss Angela
produced last night I examined and tested for fingerprints
this morning. Mrs Wilde had not touched them for some
time, but he had quite recently. He must have spied upon
her methodically and industriously, and of course there
would be no difficulty in finding a key to the Tunbridge
box. Possibly she had some inkling of this when she wrote
to her old sewing-maid and confidante asking her to burn
the letters. More likely she was terrified of their being
found and in some way incriminating her. I should say
her husband was a bitterly jealous man.

'He is extremely clever. I watched him with the closest
interest from the first. His rendering of the part of a
conscientious witness at our mock trial was quite brilliant.
His subsequent confession in the teeth of his own carefully
arranged alibi was just a little too subtle. He was trying to
play that game of bluff that goes on *ad infinitum*: "If I say I
did it, he will never believe me, or will he guess I would
reason like this, and therefore suspect me; or will he think
that I would have thought this out also as an innocent
man, and yet being determined to save my wife, also
given myself up, and am therefore not guilty." He
probably got as far as this bend in the endless and profit-
less road, and on an impulse, made his decision. You

came in beautifully with a recapitulation of his alibi and he then gave a clever impersonation of the would-be martyr foiled by facts.

'From that moment I was certain of him, but I had to clear up the Russian element, and I had to make out a case. What a case.'

Alleyn hitched his long legs on to the seat and stared up at the luggage rack.

'When I found the left-hand dogskin glove at the back of the tallboy in her bedroom and learnt that the fastening corresponded with the one I had raked out of the hall grate, I knew I was on the right track. If he had worn both gloves and destroyed them, leaving only the half-burnt button, I should have traced it and should have been tempted to suspect his wife perhaps, although I had noted his small hands. But the left-hand glove was lost behind the drawer and the left-hand print was on the banister.'

'Will they get a conviction?'

'How can I say? Remember he has already confessed once.'

'Gosh, yes! What bitter irony! But it seems to me a clever counsel—'

'Oh, quite possibly. Still, what will you all say, on oath, when questioned about his behaviour just now in my reconstruction?'

'As little as possible.'

'And how will Rosamund Grant answer when asked to say, on oath, if she told Wilde of his wife's infidelity?'

'Did she do this?'

'I am certain of it. She went for a walk with Wilde the day following the conversation she overheard between Rankin and Mrs Wilde. The gardener's child passed them and remarked that she appeared to be very agitated. I believe she regretted this piece of work and went to make a clean breast of it to Rankin in his room that night. Counsel will be certain to press this and to ask her why she would not give an account of herself. She was frightened of Wilde, of course.'

'It will be a ghastly business,' said Nigel.

'It will be unpleasant, but he is not a suitable type for liberty.'

The train shot them through a plethora of suburban backyards. Alleyn stood up and struggled into his overcoat.

'You are an extraordinary creature,' said Nigel suddenly. 'You struck me as being as sensitive as any of us just before you made the arrest. Your nerves seemed to be all anyhow. I should have said you hated the whole game. And now, an hour later, you utter inhuman paltitudes about types. You *are* a rum 'un.'

'Unspeakable juvenile! Is this your manner when interviewing the great? Come and dine with me tomorrow.'

'I say, I'd like to, but I can't. I'm taking Angela to a show.'

'Keeping company like?'

'You go to hell!'

'Well, here's Paddington.'